SABRA ZOO

find a clean T-shirt that morning. Eli wasn't pretty, not in the way that Samir would think, but there was something about her, the way she held herself, the frankness of her gaze. Several times I'd caught sight of her across a room, laughing or smiling, and I knew she was beautiful. In the few days I'd known her, I'd never seen her wear make-up, although she was partial to wearing ribbons in her hair.

'Are you two ready?' Asha asked, raising her black eyebrows at me in mock seriousness. She smiled again and my eyes were drawn to her perfectly formed white teeth; it happened every time she smiled, which she did a lot.

We stopped by the bed of an unconscious man who had a bloody bandage covering the stump where his right leg used to be. His family were standing around him, towering over Asha expectantly.

Asha prodded at his bandage. 'Tell them I had to remove his leg ...'

I waited, hoping to be able to interpret something more than the obvious.

'Tell them his leg was too damaged by the shrapnel to be saved, but that with the right prosthetic and treatment from Eli he'll be walking in several weeks.'

She waited as I struggled for the Arabic for 'prosthetic'. I settled for 'false leg' instead, although God knows I'd had to say it often enough that summer for it to be in my top ten most used words.

Asha continued, 'Because the amputation was beneath the knee he will have complete flexibility in the leg, so he was lucky in that respect.'

She smiled at the family as I translated. I asked if they had questions. The man's wife started to cry and a male relative thanked Asha, calling her 'Doctora'. She was renowned in the camp, her tireless efforts to patch people up rewarded with enormous respect by men who wouldn't have let their own sisters become doctors but would no doubt have begged to be operated on by this small Indian woman if they'd been unfortunate enough to need it.

'This boy is a sad case,' Asha said in her perfect, easy-on-the-ear English, stopping at the bed of a dark-haired kid of about twelve or thirteen, about the same age my brother Karam would have been if he was still alive. He had the same dark look about him, the same eyes, eyebrows that almost met in the middle and thick hair. He was having his dressing changed by a nurse and his black eyes flashed in anger or pain. 'His foot was badly damaged although Dr Angstrom and I managed to save it,' said Asha. A woman, maybe the boy's mother, sat by his bed, stroking his dark hair. I felt queasy as the nurse irrigated the wound with saline, running gauze through a hole in one side of his foot and out of the other. The boy moaned. Asha held his bony hand and asked the nurse how much pethidine he was on.

'More than he should be,' the nurse replied, another foreign volunteer, Scandinavian of some sort, I didn't know and it wasn't the time to inquire, although Samir would have had the name of her hotel by now, would have arranged to meet her later and take her on a tour of recent bomb sites. Asha was talking to me.

'Tell his aunt that he will need three weeks in hospital and then physiotherapy, to make sure he walks properly again.'

I translated, the Arabic for 'physiotherapy' eluding me as the sight of the wound and last night's vodka conspired to make me inarticulate. Luckily, the boy's aunt kicked in as I floundered, effusively thanking Doctora Asha.

'She said thank you,' was the best I could do; my stomach had become detached from the rest of my insides and my hands felt clammy.

'Maybe Ivan needs to lie down,' Eli said.

I ignored the jibe and was relieved to see the nurse start to dress the terrible wound. I tried to focus on the fact that the boy was now addressing me.

'Have you ever seen a wound like this?' he said, pointing at his foot. He tried to shift himself up the bed using arms that didn't look strong enough to support even his light weight.

'You're very brave,' I said. 'How did it happen?'

'We went to play football and I kicked a tin off the pitch. At least I thought it was a tin. My uncle, God rest his soul, said it was a cluster bomb.'

The boy's aunt was making her feelings about the use of cluster bombs very clear, using some strong language unusual for Palestinian women of her age. It occurred to me, not for the first time that summer, that war was liberating in many unexpected ways.

'Did you watch the World Cup?' I asked the boy, even though it was two months ago.

'Yeah, Paolo Rossi was the best, don't you think?'

'He sure was,' I said, vaguely recalling that Italy had won. 'My name is Ivan. I'll see you again soon.'

'What sort of name is Ifan?' he asked; excusable since there is no letter 'v' in the Arabic alphabet.

'It's Russian,' I told him.

He looked at me with more interest. 'Are you Russian?'

'No.' I didn't elaborate on my Danish and Palestinian roots.

'I'm Youssef,' the boy said. He extended his hand to me in a formal gesture that was touching. His skin was paper dry and his grip weak. It was like shaking the hand of a dusty skeleton in a school laboratory.

We moved on, past the maimed and the critically ill, only occasionally stopping at someone newly operated on; most people on the ward were leftovers from the violence of the summer siege of

Beirut, too ill to be discharged. Most had already been told (some by me) that they wouldn't be playing football or the piano again.

We stopped by the bed of an elderly man who had been in various hospitals since June. He was nicknamed Donkey Man by the staff because he'd broken his leg falling off a donkey, although he swore blind that he was wounded fighting in the south of Lebanon. Due to his age and wartime diet his leg was taking months to heal. The hospital was keen to discharge him but he had nowhere to go. His family had stopped visiting after the first week; no one knew why. Perhaps they'd suffered enough of his fanciful stories, although it was more likely they'd gone back south and hadn't been able to return. I suspected Donkey Man enjoyed the bed baths given by the nurses too much, and leaving would deprive him of this one pleasure.

'How are we feeling today?' Asha asked, knocking on his yellowing cast for clues.

'When will I be washed by the blonde nurse?' Donkey Man replied, not waiting for the translation.

'He's feeling fine, never felt better,' I said. I was keen to get some breakfast since my nausea had passed.

'Tell him the cast is coming off in a couple of days,' said Asha.

Asha and I went to the makeshift kitchen in the basement, leaving Eli to coax a young girl into using a newly fitted artificial leg. People were queuing up for hard-boiled eggs, sweet tea and hot flat bread. We found a seat on a box of medical supplies donated by Christian Aid and I cracked my egg on my bony knee.

'You don't look well,' Asha said. 'Are you eating properly?' This was rich coming from her. Dark rings under her eyes offset the paleness of her brown skin. Her black hair had lost the lustre it had when she'd first arrived in the city. I knew that she hadn't left the hospital in three days; the summer for her had been a constant run of traumatic amputations, relief coming only in the form of the odd dislocation or broken bone.

'I'm fine, Mother,' I said, examining the purple yolk of my extra-hard egg. I was reluctant to tell her that I'd spent an alcohol-fuelled evening with some of the other foreign volunteers and friends in my parents' apartment, my parents having left in the PLO exodus three days before. I suspected she would disapprove of such goings-on under the circumstances. Or perhaps she would understand that it was how some of her colleagues coped and would be sympathetic, although she herself never drank and avoided the expatriate crowd. She referred to them as tourists.

I first met Asha in a makeshift hospital in an office block in the Hamra district, a relatively well-heeled part of west Beirut, less prone to attracting incoming ordnance, which was why the hospital was housed there. It was July, the siege was settling nicely into a routine that people could understand: the water had been cut off, the electricity had died, the city had been pounded with big bombs, peppered with small, a ceasefire was announced and then it started all over again. Medical volunteers began to arrive from all over the world, although the Scandinavians were heavily represented. I'd been persuaded by Asha, whom I'd met through friends of my parents, to interpret for the volunteer medics crazy enough to come to this hellhole. I'd gone to meet her at the hospital but before I even had time to get my bearings a group of armed men had stormed the emergency room carrying a badly burnt comrade, bits of smoking clothes and skin falling from him. Waving their AK-47s around and shouting, they'd demanded immediate treatment. Everyone had frozen but Asha had stepped forward, her small frame blocking the men's way.

'Tell them', she said, keeping her eye squarely on the men as I cowered behind her, 'that no one comes into my emergency room with weapons.'

Without thinking, I addressed the insane-looking bunch, my voice wavering; they looked as if they hadn't had much sleep in the last week. There was a moment's silence as they looked at us, deciding whether to shoot the small foreign doctor and the sweaty kid trying to hide behind her, but then they backed away, standing outside while Asha and the others treated the injured man. Later I was given the unwanted task of telling them that their comrade was in a bad way and was unlikely to survive. The fighters, slumped in their jeep and chain-smoking, told me to apologise to the good Doctora on their behalf, to explain that they were under a lot of pressure. I went back in to the makeshift emergency room to reassure everybody that they weren't about to be shot but was sent straight back out by Asha to ask them to donate blood; I soon learnt that this was a standard request for anyone entering the hospital on their own feet. I went back the next day. I felt useful.

Now, as we finished breakfast in the canteen beneath the Sabra camp hospital, my stomach wasn't coping with my over-boiled egg.

'Are you coming to my place tonight?' I asked Asha.

'Of course,' she said. I stood up to go but had to leave without saying goodbye; hospital staff and patients' relatives quickly surrounded her, blocking her from my view.

What Asha didn't know, and I would never tell her, was that I had to get back to Hamra to courier some forged papers. That was why I'd been asked to stay in the city rather than leave on a ship with my parents. I felt for the reason in my back pocket – my Danish passport, which allowed me relatively easy movement around the city. The war was over and I was parent-free for the first time, with my own apartment. I couldn't ask for more.

2

I made my way down Hamra Street, heading to Samir's café before my rendezvous at the forging house. Hamra Street was the main shopping street of west Beirut and dissected the area of the same name. It was only slightly scarred by shelling compared to the southern reaches of west Beirut, where the refugee camps and the multitude of abandoned PLO offices were situated. This was a more affluent west Beirut, where boutiques, cinemas and street cafés occupied the ground floors of large apartment blocks, many empty as the owners had left for Europe or the east of the city. Since the siege had eased, goods were getting in and there were more people on the street, doing more everyday things; I passed a hairdressing salon in which women sat in curlers, and a café where men sat on the pavement outside drinking coffee and smoking narghilehs. Samir's place – consisting of a food counter and a few Formica tables – was next to the cinema where only a few months ago I'd watched *Mad Max* with my schoolmates, unaware of our own impending apocalypse. It was a good place to stop if I thought I was being followed, but it was also a good place to eat. Samir was often found there, supervising the making of his 'special' falafel mix and blending the secret sauce he served with it himself (he wouldn't trust anyone else with the formula). He had managed to keep the place open even during the worst of the siege. I usually ate there for nothing when Samir was on the premises. He would greet the regulars and swap the latest rumours while casting his eye over any woman that passed the shop front. He had a radar for them.

'Ivan,' he called from behind the counter, his neatly pressed clothes protected by an apron, 'the situation must be improving – the women are starting to look like women again.'

I watched Samir fill flat bread with some wilting salad and freshly fried falafel but stopped him dribbling his secret sauce over the top.

'He's no fool, this one,' said one of the customers, laughing.

'You won't be laughing when it's being sold in every shop across the Middle East,' Samir said.

This just provoked more laughter and he handed the sandwich to me with a hurt expression. I bit into it hungrily, listening to the banter. It was all about the PLO leaving and what would happen now.

'So,' one of them was asking, 'you think the Israelis will enter the city?'

'For sure, they'll want to check for themselves that the PLO has left,' someone said.

'Not with the multinationals here. Not with the Americans at the port,' said another.

'What, and the multinational force is going to be here for ever? They only came for the evacuation, you idiot.'

And so the discussion went, everyone giving their prediction on when the Western troops would leave. I knew that most of these Lebanese men, Samir among them, had ambivalent feelings about the PLO. Although they may have earnt their money working for them (like Samir, claiming he'd driven Arafat himself) they were also relieved that they had gone. The feeling was that the Palestinians had overstayed their welcome in Lebanon since arriving in 1967, turning parts of it into a permanent home from home. My Timex told me I was going to be late if I didn't move.

Five minutes from Samir's place I turned south off Hamra Street onto Rue Descartes, and picking my way past a shoulder-high mountain of rotting garbage entered a 1930s apartment block. An old lady in glasses was checking the mailboxes. She caught sight of me before I got to the stairs.

'Who are you? You don't live here,' she said.

'Just visiting, Auntie. Don't worry yourself.'

'Visiting who?'

I took the stairs three at a time to the third floor. I knocked with a pre-arranged tattoo on the door and grinned at the eye that darkened the security peephole. Najwa let me into the apartment and bolted the door behind me. Her once tight-fitting jeans hung from her hips like a denim skirt.

'You're late,' she said in Arabic, limping towards the dining-room table where official papers and rubber stamps lay carefully arranged. My mother once told me that Najwa had spent three months in a Syrian prison and had come out with a limp and a streak of white on one side of her jet-black hair.

'I'm here now,' I said.

'Spending too much time with those foreign nurses?' she asked, smirking.

I felt my face redden but didn't answer; smirking women were not something I'd yet learnt to deal with. I knew that she didn't want to spend more than an hour in the place, as there was a chance it could be raided. Today wasn't the first time the neighbours had questioned one of us in the lobby. Our story was that we were watering the plants until the owners came back.

She sat back at the table, sticking a passport photo of a young man onto a blank Israeli travel permit. I watched as she impressed the photo with a home-made rubber stamp. It was similar to one of several I had helped to make just a couple of weeks before. They were made from the official stamps on legitimate documents borrowed (or indeed stolen) from sympathetic people who could travel through Israeli lines. The forging operation was originally housed in a windowless basement with a steel door in the south of the city, and was run by another foreign volunteer, a cheery German called Andreas who was rumoured to be an ex-member of the Baader-Meinhof group and who had an artificial left hand. Whatever the truth, in short supply in the fever of a summer war, he'd shown me how to create a rubber stamp from a facsimile and how to remove a signature from a passport using only what could be bought in a stationery shop. Andreas had acquired his rubber-coated left hand after putting together a letter bomb which detonated before it could be posted. Since the PLO evacuation a few days ago, which took Andreas with it (keffiyah and large sunglasses conveniently covering his fair head), the operation had been split up into smaller discrete parts, each occupying a different dwelling across the city. This apartment was one of them. It was unoccupied, its owners having left for France, entrusting the keys to Najwa, whose handbag was weighed down with several sets. It was unclear to me how she remembered which keys opened what door or how indeed she explained having so many on her. She must have told people she was watering a lot of plants.

She gave me three complete forged travel permits. I wrapped and taped them in a sheet of paper then taped the package inside the day's newspaper with the headline 'INTERNAL SECURITY FORCES DEPLOYED IN SOUTHERN SUBURBS', and folded the paper in three.

'Any new volunteers we should know about?' Najwa asked, sitting back in her chair and putting her hands behind her head. My eyes were momentarily drawn to the hair under her armpits, which was a different colour from the mainly jet-black hair on her head. She noticed my gaze and folded her arms. I felt like I'd been caught looking down her blouse.

'There are a couple of new nurses and a new Belgian doctor,' I replied, studying the criss-cross sticky tape on the windowpanes, designed to stop it shattering into fragments and shredding the occupants in the event of an explosion.

'Have you got names?' she asked.

I reluctantly muttered their names, which she wrote down. 'What are you going to do with those, run them through the PLO super-computer?' I said. Surprised by my own sarcasm, my face flushed again.

'This is serious, Ivan, this isn't a game. Those of us who have remained behind are at risk. Not everyone has a foreign passport to fall back on.'

I wanted to say something about her being able to make one for herself but held my tongue. During the summer I'd talked of burning my Danish passport after similar jibes from people, but my mother had told me not to be stupid. Najwa tried to conceal the effort of getting up from the table and started to gather the stamps and passes together, avoiding my eyes. 'Let's meet again in three days, my place,' she said.

'What time? I don't want to be late.'

She gave me a look.

I made my way back onto the street, tensing in the September sun, patting my tatty passport still sitting snug in my hip pocket. I walked the four kilometres to the American University Hospital, where people who could pay went to get better. At the reception I asked for a Dr Ramina and was put through to her on the phone.

'Hello, it's George,' I said, trying to ignore the look of curiosity on the receptionist's face. 'I've come for my blood test results.' I found myself talking English with a slight Arabic accent, taking on the less than perfect cadence of Dr Ramina. It was something I did when I spoke to Samir in English, or indeed when I spoke English to a Norwegian. Maybe it was a subconscious need to be accepted.

Dr Ramina's office was off one side of a laboratory where technicians sat at benches looking through microscopes. Dr Ramina looked middle-aged or just tired – it was difficult to tell in those post-siege days. She had lipstick on her teeth.

'So, you've come for your results, George?' she said in an unnaturally loud voice. She pretended to inquire about my parents, whom she'd never met, while she dug out a patient's file from a stack on her desk and made a show of consulting it. I put my newspaper on the desk, next to an identical one, except, I noticed, it wasn't folded in the same way.

'Everything looks fine, I think the iron tablets are working. Your red cell count is back to normal.'

'OK, good,' I said, standing up. 'I do feel a lot better.' I picked up her newspaper from the desk and folded it in three as we walked out to the corridor together. We stood waiting for the lift and I wished she would leave; it wasn't normal to be standing out here with me, a healthy person, when she had real patients to see. She leant towards me and spoke in a low voice: 'To be honest, maybe you should have a blood test, you do look anaemic.'

I stepped into the lift and smiled at her as the doors closed.

Later that night I was in what I now called my apartment. I wasn't sure who it belonged to but it was where my parents had moved after having to evacuate our own apartment earlier in the summer. A group sat round the large coffee table covered in half-empty wine bottles and full ashtrays. It was dark outside but I'd lost track of the time. Samir had brought a couple of Lebanese friends whom I didn't know. They weren't drinking but chain-smoked Marlboros. They both had moustaches and one of them was in the process of growing a beard.

Samir was talking over Don McLean on the turntable. 'Did anyone see the US marines at the port?' he asked. 'You need to go and see them, they're very short.'

'They're what?' asked a Swedish woman whose name I couldn't remember. She was easily the oldest person there and spoke the least English. I wasn't sure if we'd been introduced but I thought she was an anaesthetist. She didn't look comfortable, perched on the end of her chair.

'Short,' Samir said, holding his hand up to indicate. 'Small, like this.'

I had noticed this when I'd followed the departing convoy of PLO fighters to the port, where they'd boarded ships to be dispersed around the Mediterranean. I'd walked alongside them from the municipal stadium where they embarked, saying goodbye to my mother, who was standing in a truck with other wives of cadres along with some trusted comrades to look after them. They'd been dressed in brand-new fatigues and keffiyahs, like everyone else. The fighters triumphantly shot rounds from their AK-47s into the air. Hot bullet casings had stung the side of my head; later Asha told me that many people had come into hospital with head injuries caused by falling bullet shells. She wasn't pleased at this unnecessary extra work. I'd reached the roadblock at the port, where the US marines were stationed, letting through the trucks full of armed PLO fighters in battle dress. They did look short and nervous, but maybe that was because everyone else was standing in trucks. That was when I'd unexpectedly spotted my father, incongruously dressed in fatigues and helmet, sporting an AK-47 and sitting in the front of a truck, next to the driver. He looked awkward and out of place. I'd jumped up onto the running board and tried to give him a hug, but the weapon and helmet got in the way. I was pulled down and my father disappeared through the roadblock. All through the siege I'd hardly seen him. I felt cheated by our wordless and inept farewell.

We drank some more and I made a toast to the short marines, before stopping someone from picking at the deposited wax on an empty Chianti bottle that had been used as a candleholder. I'd been nurturing it all summer, even bringing it with me when we moved to this apartment from our previous home.

'What about the Italians?' someone else said. 'Have you seen their hats?' It was true that the Italian contingent had worn ridiculous headgear; tall and feathered, they looked like they'd just come from being on parade in front of the Vatican. The war-hardened kids in the camps couldn't believe it – these guys had come to protect them? Only the French paratroopers looked like a real fighting force. Big, tough-looking men with shaved heads, people wished they'd been there during the siege. Another toast to the Italians was followed by one to the paratroopers. Samir and his teetotal friends started talking about the pros and cons of the different weapons the multinational forces carried.

Bored, I went to the kitchen where Eli and Asha were making something to eat. John, the paediatrician from Scotland, was there. He was popular with the camp inhabitants but some of his colleagues were ambivalent about his presence, even questioning the time I spent interpreting for him in his clinic. I thought it must have something to do with him coming to Beirut on his own rather than through a charity. Najwa had been particularly interested in John when I told her about him. You couldn't tell who had entered the city, she said; it was more difficult to check people out since the PLO apparatus had been dismantled. Having seen him in his clinic it was difficult to imagine that he was anything other than a doctor but people were always wary of someone they couldn't easily pigeonhole. He was making a tomato sauce to go with the spaghetti on the stove.

'Ivan, Dostoyevsky or Tolstoy?' he asked, as if offering a choice of fruit.

I pretended to mull it over. 'Dostoyevsky, I think.' I'd never read Tolstoy.

He nodded and his glasses steamed up under his curly hair. He made Asha laugh, saying, 'You're making me hot, baby.' It was funny because no one else would dare say that to her. I was sick of spaghetti; it was all we had eaten over the summer, along with rice, lentils, tinned tuna and sardines. All the lights went out and a collective groan came from the living room. In the kitchen, lit only by the blue flame on the stove, there was a practised scramble to light candles. I was standing close to Eli.

'I need your help with the boy, Youssef, the one with the foot injury,' she said to me. Her eyes flickered in the candlelight. Her braid was undone and her brown hair held back with a band.

'Of course,' I said. Helping with Youssef would be a good excuse to spend time with her, although I thought the boy could do with some extra support. 'I can come down to the hospital tomorrow.' We swapped smiles.

'So this is your apartment?' she asked.

'It is, since my parents left, although it's not theirs either, the owners are in London. We only came here in the summer because it was safer during the bombing.'

'Ivan's bachelor pad. Better watch yourself, lassie,' John said.

'Where are they, your parents?' she asked.

'They've gone ... on a ... um, cruise.'

'A cruise?'

'Yes. They thought it was time they saw the Mediterranean.'

She couldn't tell whether her leg was being pulled. Smiling, I headed back to the living room.

The mood was quieter. Don McLean had been silenced by the power cut.

'Where is your husband?' one of Samir's friends asked the anaesthetist, lighting a Marlboro from one already going.

'He's with my daughter, at home in Sweden,' she answered, cradling a glass of wine to her chest.

'Mother should be with daughter,' he said smiling, but his lips had thinned.

'She's almost a woman now and I will be back with her soon.' She smiled as if visualising the moment.

'Haven't you heard of women's lib?' laughed Liv, a black-haired Norwegian who called herself a Trotskyist. I wasn't sure what that was beyond a love of Trotsky, but the label suited her for some reason. I knew (through listening to my father) that Leninists hated Trotsky but I wasn't sure why.

'Why you are coming here?' asked the man, louder than before. His question was aimed at the wider group but the anaesthetist was taken aback. Her mouth twitched nervously. She and Liv exchanged a look. I hoped Samir would intervene, but he'd disappeared onto the balcony with someone.

'They've come to help us,' I said, immediately thinking how feeble this sounded.

'We don't want their help,' Marlboro Man said, gesturing to the now silent gathering with his burning cigarette. 'Foreigners have created the problems here, more of them will not make it better. We Arabs can solve our own problems.'

'I don't remember', Samir said in Arabic, as he stepped in from the balcony, 'seeing any Arabs here when we needed their help. Where were your fucking Arabs when we were being bombed by F-16s and shelled by gunboats?'

Marlboro Man's companion, the one trying to grow the beard, addressed Samir in Arabic. 'You are trying to be Western, Samir, listening to this shit,' pointing at the records, 'drinking alcohol, spending time with decadent Western women. You are a blasphemer. You should be a true Muslim.'

I started to laugh, but saw that the man's hands were shaking and that neither he nor his companion was laughing. Samir, though, was smiling at this outburst. I picked up someone's packet of Kent from the table but didn't think I could light one without making a hash of it. This wasn't how I'd envisaged the evening.

'Maybe your friends should leave', I said to Samir in Arabic, not looking at the men, 'if they don't feel comfortable with our guests.'

'They are just going, I think,' Samir said, still smiling, moving towards them. Asha entered the room carrying a pan of spaghetti, trailing steam. As the two men stood up I saw a flash of candle-lit blue steel under Marlboro Man's jacket. I glanced at the housing for the rolling shutter above the balcony door, where I'd hidden my own ancient Soviet-made Tokarev 9mm automatic on the last day of the PLO evacuation.

Asha put the pan on the table and was followed into the room by Eli and John, carrying plates and cutlery. The two men pushed by them into the hall, followed by Samir.

'Let's eat,' said Asha, as Eli handed out plates, looking quizzically at me.

I shrugged, just glad they were leaving.

'Let's drink,' John said, raising a glass of wine he'd chosen from a selection on the table.

The front door closed and Samir came back into the room smiling and stroking his moustache.

'Who were they?' Liv asked. 'They seem so – what's the word – serious.'

'They used to be fun guys,' Samir said, 'but they discovered God during the summer.'

'And I thought God had died during the summer,' said John, draining his glass.

3

I stood outside the camp hospital with the official interpreter, smoking and swapping funny patient stories. We watched an old man push a cart past, stacked precariously with cages of chickens. She stood very close to me when she spoke, touching me on the arm with blood-red fingernails, the polish chipped at the tips. She smelt of jasmine, and a small tuft of blonde hair had escaped from her ponytail at the base of the neck. I could see the dark roots coming through at her scalp. I could also see a small gold cross resting deep in her cleavage. My reverie was broken by John's voice.

'Hey Ivan – hey, lover boy,' he shouted from the entrance, 'I need you in the clinic.'

Because the war was now supposed to be over, children had started reclaiming their usual illnesses.

The clinic was full of women with kids crying, laughing or just being quietly pale. It was these silent ones, the lacklustre, curled up on their mothers' laps, who John asked the Palestinian nurse to triage first. This system encouraged more noise outside the examination room as worried mothers tried to be seen first, holding up crying babies as proof of priority. I had a flashback to a few days before: women holding up babies and toddlers to armed men in trucks, telling them, 'Kiss your father goodbye.' I wondered how many families in the camp were now without their menfolk. John got me to speak directly to the children, bypassing their mothers' unsolicited lists of symptoms and diagnoses.

'If she already knows what's wrong, ask her why she's here,' he would say to me in a Scottish accent strong enough to need internal deciphering. I didn't translate these pointed comments, sticking instead to the purely clinical. John was at ease in the refugee camp, claiming that it was no more horrendous than some of the Glaswegian tenements in which he cut his teeth as a general practitioner, adding that they probably ate better here, even during the siege.

'Mothers are the same everywhere,' he would say. 'They just want what's best for their children.'

We worked through a string of minor infections, wounds that wouldn't heal and diarrhoea from dirty water. Then the nurse brought in a boy, a young teenager who had come alone. He had a painful and bloated stomach. He was reluctant to answer questions and was eventually coaxed into having a rectal examination after some painful prodding of his swollen belly. John probed with a latexed finger, looking into the middle distance in concentration.

'I think we'll need to get him onto the ward,' he said, snapping rubber into a bin.

I translated and the boy started to cry.

'It'll be OK,' John said to him gently, patting his head.

Later, in the children's ward, John was pulling pistachio nut after pistachio nut from the boy's rectum. I didn't understand what had happened to him. The stench was unbearable and I withdrew to the corridor, listening to the other bedridden kids in the ward complaining about the smell.

'Ivan, some abuses are the same the world over; these things must have been up here several days – it's like opening the bloody floodgates,' John shouted from behind the curtains.

I made for the orthopaedic ward, his mad laugh receding. I found Eli at Youssef's bedside.

'Hello Youssef, remember me?' I asked, standing on the opposite side of the bed to Eli. Youssef looked away. He seemed frail and helpless, his bare chest sunken.

'He won't cooperate,' she said, holding up crutches. 'He needs to start getting about on his own.'

So far Youssef had been carried everywhere as there was no wheelchair small enough for him.

'What's the plan?' I asked Eli, noticing freckles in the V-neck of her white top.

I carried Youssef into the corridor, taking him to the end furthest from the ward, as instructed by Eli. He was worryingly light and bony; it was like carrying a large bird. I set him down on his good foot and he collapsed onto his backside. With his back against the wall, he stuck his bandaged football of a foot out along the floor. Eli tried to hand him the crutches.

'No!' he shouted in English.

'Tell him he needs to try to walk to me,' she said, laying the crutches on the floor next to him.

I sat down next to Youssef, stretching out my legs. I was thirsty. The smell of week-old excrement sought us out. The marble floor was cool to the touch. We watched Eli walk to the other end of the corridor.

'You like her, yes?' Youssef said in English, his eyes still on Eli as she stood to face us, gesturing for Youssef to come to her.

'Yes, of course I do, don't you?' I said, knowing what was coming.

'No, I mean you love her.' He giggled. 'You want to fickety fick her?'

I felt my ears grow hot. Was I that obvious? 'Shame on you,' I said. 'She's married, with a son as old as you.' The marriage bit was no longer true, according to Samir, who'd heard it from Liv, but I wasn't getting into that with Youssef.

'I can't walk all that way,' he said, switching to Arabic and pointing down the hall at Eli.

'Try to go just half way then,' I said.

'Not even half way.' He folded his arms and set his mouth hard. I shook my head at Eli and picked Youssef up, carrying him back to the ward and placing him in his bed.

'We'll try again tomorrow,' Eli said, smiling at Youssef.

I took Eli aside. 'I'm not sure how useful I can be, I'm just an interpreter,' I said.

'And I'm just a physiotherapist,' she said. 'Anyway, he'll do better with a male influence.'

'If you think so.'

She smiled. 'Yes, I do.'

I wanted to ask whether I was going to see her that night but Youssef was grinning and winking at me and I left before he said something embarrassing.

On my way out an English surgeon in sweat-stained scrubs collared me. He wasn't one of my usual charges. He was tall with fair stubble and eyes bloodshot with tiredness or alcohol. I nodded, looking at my watch. I had to do a fake ID run in a couple of hours. We entered the post-op area and stopped at the end of the bed of a beefy man with bandaged eyes and hands. He was propped up, his face and chest peppered with small fresh wounds. There was dried blood on his pillow and no one by his bedside.

'This man is a cluster bomb victim, picked the fucking thing up to get rid of it and it exploded in his face.' The doctor took a deep breath. 'We operated on his eyes but we haven't got a decent eye man here.'

I looked at the doctor for a moment and felt my armpits prickle with sweat.

'Are you telling me he's blind?' I asked.

'Yes, and he doesn't know yet.'

'Where's his family? I usually give bad news to the family, I don't usually do it straight to the patient.'

'You'll be fine, the other interpreter, the girl, would be here but she prefers the glamour of working with a TV film crew.'

I smiled to myself; I'd turned down the opportunity to interpret on the film the British crew were making about the hospital. Now I had to pay the price.

We approached the bedside; I needed a drink of water.

'Sir, can you hear me?' I asked the man in Arabic. The bandaged head turned towards me. 'I'm with the doctor.' I realised that I didn't know the doctor's name. 'I'm with the doctor who operated on you.'

The man nodded in recognition. 'Dr Boulos,' he said, the Arabic for 'Paul'. Dr Paul placed his hand on the man's forearm.

'Dr Boulos operated on your eyes but there is a problem, I mean it was difficult, the eyes are delicate and ...' I paused, trying to think of the right words to tell him. The bandages turned towards me again. The doctor's hand was clenched round the man's wrist. 'How does one say?' I said to myself.

'You have already said it,' the man said.

'I'm sorry.' I was apologising for my own ineptitude rather than the fact that the man was blind. 'Do you have questions for the doctor?'

'Thank him for me,' the man said. He sounded very tired.

Going down the stairs to the lobby I heard shouting and was surprised to see that it was Asha. She was addressing a white male doctor who was with a group of new medics, gesturing at the families of refugees camped in the lobby, whose number had been growing daily since the PLO evacuation.

'These people have every right to be here,' she was saying. 'This is their hospital, not yours, it doesn't belong to the doctors and it isn't for you to tell them they shouldn't be here.' The medics exchanged raised eyebrows. 'You're not lording it over the natives here, nor do you have the same dubious status you may have back in London.'

The hospital administrator bustled into the lobby – a fearsome woman who disapproved of my presence in her hospital. I was only tolerated on site because of John and Asha's insistence that I was useful.

Asha continued in forced moderation, her voice quieter. 'The infrastructure has collapsed ... Imagine if one day you woke up and the government had packed up and left. That's what's happened here.' She pulled a young refugee girl to her, who looked scared, which wasn't surprising since Doctora Asha's interest in people usually involved pain. 'This girl's father has left, been forced out, and these people are worried, they are no longer protected. They don't feel safe.' Asha stopped, letting her shoulders droop. The administrator was leading the group of puzzled-looking medics away, saying something about it having been a difficult summer in which they'd been short-staffed.

Welcome to Sabra, I thought. Asha was left standing in the lobby holding the girl's hand. The girl was trying to work herself free. Asha looked at her in surprise, apologised and let her go. She spotted me and came towards me. Her eyes were filling with tears.

'I can't be seen like this,' she said, her voice low and cracking. I walked with her out onto the street. I could see Samir laughing with the official interpreter and the BBC TV film crew. Having asked Asha to wait at the entrance, I walked up to him, pulling on his sleeve.

'I need you to drive Asha home,' I said in Arabic so the others couldn't understand.

'Now?' he said, frowning at the interruption. A group of kids had gathered round the cameraman shouting, 'We show you bomb, you photo bomb!'

'Listen, these people are from the BBC. They want to do a story about one of the kids in the hospital. I told them about that boy Youssef you mentioned,' Samir said.

'This is not the time,' I said, pointing at Asha. The kids tugged at the cameraman's sleeve and trousers.

'The thing is,' said an English woman to me, as if I'd been part of the conversation all along, 'that we want to try and get one of the kids flown to the UK for treatment, make a story of it, something the British public can identify with.' She was wearing a safari jacket with lots of pockets; I assumed she must be the producer or director.

'You'd need to ask Youssef and his mother,' I said. I pulled again at Samir's sleeve, muttering in Arabic, 'We need to take Asha back.' The cameraman was trying to swat the kids away. They were now asking five lira to show him their bomb. They may have been the same boys who suckered another journalist into filming a Coke can they'd painted yellow, claiming it was a cluster bomb.

'The thing is,' continued the producer, exchanging a fleeting look with the official interpreter, 'I understand this Youssef boy might be ah … a bit difficult and may not come across well on TV but that the girl with the prosthetic might be more suitable ah … from a visual point of view.' The girl in question was one the official interpreter looked after, fair-haired, green-eyed and practically mute. Youssef was dark-haired, dark-eyed and said 'fickety fick'.

'We have to go,' I said to Samir in an urgent whisper, ignoring the producer who turned to talk to the official interpreter.

Samir looked at Asha waiting at the entrance. 'Why didn't you say something?' he said, pulling out his keys.

Soon we were riding in what Samir told me was a 1979 Series 7 BMW used to ferry top PLO cadres around the city. He looked at Asha in the mirror.

'The old man used to sit there,' he said.

'The old man?' she asked, her first words since getting into the car.

I turned round. She looked small on the large leather seat.

'He means Yasser Arafat.'

Asha didn't want to go back to her hotel in case she had to speak to anyone so Samir dropped us outside my place. He leant from the driver's window and held out a business card. 'Listen, this guy works for a TV news company, I do some driving for him sometimes. He's looking for an interpreter. They pay in dollars.'

I pocketed the card without looking at it.

'You need to sleep,' I told Asha, once we were inside. I tried to find clean linen for my bed. She followed me into the bedroom.

'Who has slept in this bed?' she asked.

'Only me.'

'Then don't worry about changing the sheets.'

She started to get undressed and I left the room, closing the door.

'Don't go,' she said. Something had happened to her voice. I went back in, saw her standing in a slip, her small frame illuminated by slats of light from the closed shutters. Her tears came freely and it seemed right that I go to her. I held her to my chest, felt the wetness through my T-shirt, the racking of her little body. Eventually the sobs subsided but I was still stroking her long wiry hair. She lifted her head back and looked at me smiling, her face wet but happy.

'I couldn't have done that in front of anyone else here,' she said, placing her hands on my face. I could feel an erection growing. Mortified, I moved my groin back so she couldn't feel it against her. What was wrong with me? She kissed me quickly on the lips. My heart was trying to jump out of my chest, like someone had injected adrenalin directly into it. She got into bed and I went to leave the room but she called my name again. I stopped at the door to look back at her looking at me from under the sheet. I waited, heart thumping.

'Thanks again, Ivan,' she said.

I waited outside for a couple of minutes until the sound of snoring, incompatible with someone her size, came through the door. She was clearly exhausted. Thirty minutes later I was sitting on the sofa, my Tokarev on the coffee table. I lit the candle in my Chianti bottle, watching the wax flow down the neck, wondering if it was cheating to light it during the day. I started to strip my gun, carefully cleaning each part. I wasn't sure why I had done that – waited outside the door. I began to polish individual bullets before loading them back into the cartridge. I reassembled the museum piece, making sure the safety was on, and wrapped it in its greasy cloth before putting it back in its hiding place, praying that she hadn't noticed my erection.

4

I sat on Najwa's balcony smoking a Marlboro while she made Turkish or Arabic coffee – I could never remember what the difference was, something to do with how many times you brought it to the boil. Her apartment had good views of the city but faced east Beirut, which meant it was vulnerable to shells launched from there. She'd been lucky though. Over the summer destruction had come from all directions – the sky, the sea and the cedar-covered mountains overlooking the city – but her apartment had remained unscathed. Najwa brought out the small cups of coffee and sat beside me. She took one of my cigarettes.

'You smoke too much,' she said, taking her first drag and blowing blue smoke up into blue sky. I was trying to think of a way I could arrange to have lunch or dinner with Eli alone. Najwa's voice interrupted my thoughts.

'Unfortunately a couple of our people have disappeared and we've had to move cadres into new safe houses.'

I pulled on my cigarette. 'What do you mean, disappeared?' I asked, trying not to sound too nervous.

'One of them we know has deserted for Syria to join his family. The other ... Well, we think he was picked up at a flying roadblock,' she said.

'Phalangists?'

'Yes, they've started to venture over from the east.'

I sipped the bitter coffee. The war was obviously not over but had just shifted its emphasis. It seemed that staying behind in Beirut might not be the comfortable choice I had hoped it would be.

'What I am trying to say', said Najwa, 'is that we need to courier messages between cadres and ... Well, you can travel around without a problem.'

Unless I was caught with incriminating papers, I thought. Najwa handed me an envelope: I was to meet someone outside the main cafeteria of the American University with whom I was to exchange envelopes. I finished my coffee and headed for the street.

In the doorway of Najwa's building I lit another cigarette. According to Najwa, the Phalangists were making lightning raids into west Beirut to mount roadblocks and search buildings, presumably looking for known activists, Palestinians or Lebanese, anyone who had the gall to put up any resistance to the siege. The militiamen would stop a car and sometimes a hooded informer (I imagined he was on a commission) would look inside and point to anyone he vaguely recognised. I'd once seen photographs at a macabre exhibition of people after they'd fallen into the hands of Christian militias; their faces were pulp, their eyes swollen shut. I checked for my passport and started out, thinking at least it was safer on foot.

Over the years my anxiety had moved through a spectrum of fears. A spate of car bombs meant walking the streets took on a new twist: scanning parked cars for extra aerials and crossing the road to avoid being decapitated by a flying piece of metal. With rockets I had learnt (during the Civil War) to recognise the particular pre-impact whine of different calibre shells. It was said that if you could hear it coming then it had passed over and you were OK, as long as you hit the ground, keeping your chest raised to avoid being winded by the blast. Being buried alive under rubble was a new worry, thanks to the size of the bombs being dropped during the summer siege, some big enough to bring down a six-storey building. Rumours also circulated of a new vacuum bomb, which made buildings implode, turning them into neat piles of debris. Consequently, taking shelter in the basement, the place to be during a raid, became as much of a risk as staying on the top floor; in other words you chose your own odds. The list of things to be afraid of went on: snipers that made certain crossings more interesting, armed flare-ups at minor traffic incidents, guns going off by accident, and so on.

Through the gate into the American University of Beirut, or AUB as it was naturally known, was another world lined with palm trees. People my own age wandered around with books, chatting and laughing, even holding hands with the opposite sex – same-sex friends holding hands was not an uncommon sight in Beirut. I found the cafeteria but was early so I decided to go inside. It was an hour before lunch but already a hubbub came from the crowded tables, filling the vaulted ceiling. I was filled with an air of expectancy, as if I could have been a part of all this. But the feeling soon passed and I rose to leave, not wanting to be reminded that this was what I should have been doing, sitting with my peers discussing which modules I was going to take and which girl I was going to ask out. I heard someone call my name and looked over to see three of my former classmates sitting at one of the tables. I walked over feeling self-conscious, the envelope in my inside pocket digging into my ribs.

'We'd wondered what had become of you,' said Emile, standing up to shake my hand rather formally. Curly haired, green-eyed and good-looking, Emile had been the school heart-throb. I sat down and shook hands with Mustapha and Bedrosian, two stocky guys who could have been in their forties, already wearing their fathers' jackets and moustaches, being groomed to take over the import-export businesses, their mothers feeding them to develop their father's paunches.

'What course are you doing?' asked Bedrosian, stroking his moustache in a practised way. It wasn't a question I was ready for.

'I'm not decided,' I said, but a buried memory of a pre-invasion schoolroom discussion surfaced. 'Probably physics.'

'You'll need to get a move on, the deadline for applications is the end of the week,' said Mustapha, looking at me as if I was moronic.

'Where did you go this summer?' Bedrosian asked. 'We've just returned from Paris.'

'Nowhere, we stayed here.'

There were noises of disbelief.

'You mean you were here all through the siege?' This from Emile, studying me carefully with his green eyes. 'Why, for God's sake? Didn't you even go to east Beirut?'

I wasn't about to explain that I'd spent most of the summer working military radios in a basement in the Fakhani district, a no-go area for these people, who probably celebrated the PLO evacuation with champagne and canapés. Nor would I tell them that my parents had left dressed in military fatigues and that I myself had stayed on to help those left secretly behind. They'd known nothing about me before the summer; they were just one part of a compartmentalised life. I shrugged, rescued by the passing of a well-endowed girl in a tight top. I listened as they exchanged ideas about what they would like to do to her. I checked my watch.

'So what courses are you guys doing?' I said, although I could have guessed.

'Medicine,' said Emile.

'Business studies,' said Mustapha.

'Yeah, business studies,' said Bedrosian.

Outside the cafeteria, I looked for my contact, the one-time driver of a senior PLO official I'd met once over the summer. We'd had a run-in when I, operating the radios in my Signals basement, had asked him to maintain radio silence due to an impending air raid. The guy had turned up in the radio room twenty minutes later feeling that he'd been humiliated in front of his cadre who had been in the back seat of his car at the time. We'd squared up to each other, cadre's driver and cadre's son. Luckily for me, who you were related to beat who you worked for every time. His parting shot at the time was that being in Signals was an easy option for the relatives of cadres or those who couldn't do anything more useful. He was probably right, judging by everyone else who worked there, although towards the end of the summer it was one of the last PLO offices left in Fakhani. He wasn't difficult to spot, with his lazy right eye, pot belly and greying hair. They couldn't have chosen anyone less able to blend in as a student. I caught his good eye and he sneered at me. I wandered away from the crowd beginning to congregate for lunch. I found a bench off the main thoroughfare that overlooked the Mediterranean and lit a cigarette. Lazy Eye sat next to me and we gazed out at an Israeli gunboat in the distance. I could smell the sweat on him, although it could have been mine.

'May I see your newspaper?' I asked, almost adding 'comrade' at the end. He handed me the Arabic paper whose headline read 'MULTINATIONAL FORCE TO LEAVE BY 14 SEPTEMBER'. I opened it up and pulled out the envelope inside, placing it in my inside pocket and replacing it with the one I was carrying. All this was done with the newspaper open in front of me. I pretended to read the paper for another thirty seconds or so and then folded it and handed it back with a 'thanks'. We sat there for a few seconds while I waited for him to leave.

'So who are you still in contact with?' he asked.

I stood up without looking at him, walking away. I walked for a while, enjoying the trees and the sea in the distance, almost forgetting the rubble, the dust, the refugee camp, the smell of the hospital.

On my way out I saw a sign for the admissions office and stepped inside where I picked up an application form from the woman behind the desk. If nothing else, I thought, it gave the impression that I was here for a reason.

After dropping the envelope off at Najwa's I walked to the Commodore Hotel to follow the lead Samir had given me. This was another discrete compartment of my life, something I hadn't told Najwa about. The Commodore was where journalists stayed, some never leaving the confines of the hotel and its surroundings. Many of the news agencies were housed in the immediate vicinity, which meant that it was possible to string together a story based on interviews held in the bar and then wire news through without having to go anywhere too dangerous. Checking the business card Samir had given me, I found the entrance of TeleNews, situated next to the hotel. Inside I asked for Bob. I was directed into the editing room, where banks of small monitors lined a wall. A tall bearded bear of a man with dirty glasses and a ponytail was fast-forwarding video footage using a large dial on the editing desk. People walked in silent-film mode on the screen, jerking and jabbering in high-pitched voices to camera. A press of the dial froze an old man in a dirty keffiyah talking to the camera. Bob stood up to shake my hand and introduce himself. His American accent was mellow and smooth, unlike some I'd heard. His hair and beard were mostly grey and he had deep grooves in his face.

'Thanks for doing this, by the way,' he said, digging a cold beer from a small cooler under the editing desk. 'Samir said you may be able to help us out. Our usual interpreter has disappeared.'

'It's the latest craze,' I said, taking a swig from the beer and ignoring Bob's quizzical look. The immediate effect of the alcohol reminded me that I hadn't eaten all day. I translated footage for a while, helping Bob to put together a story on how people were surviving day to day post-PLO departure. He'd included some footage of the camp hospital, doing a ward round with Asha.

'She's quite a lady.' Bob nodded at the screen as Asha explained the cause of yet another mutilation. I nodded, thinking of her crying in my room. A glaring, angry Youssef replaced her on the small screen. I was surprised when Bob kept the shot of him in his piece.

In return for my help Bob offered to buy me lunch at the Commodore. His girlfriend Stacy, a freelance reporter with the same ponytail and laid-back twang as Bob, joined us. I'd never seen anyone more beautiful. She looked like a Hollywood star.

'Did you have a good siege?' she asked with a beam that created dimples in her cheeks. Her voice was gravelly and she smelt of menthol cigarettes. I couldn't stop looking at her; she had a smile you wanted to keep seeing, which she flashed at me throughout lunch whenever she caught me gawping. Her T-shirt read 'I Survived the Siege of Beirut – 1982'. I felt relaxed in their company, even confessing my half-imagined plans to go to university.

Three bottles of beer and a hotel beefburger later I was promising Bob to go out filming with him and act as interpreter. The beer distorted my reality; I daydreamt of spending time working with Bob and Stacy. Then it was just Stacy.

'You can do the sound at the same time, there's nothing to it,' Bob was saying as we stood up. 'Earn yourself a few tax-free dollars too.' We all laughed and shook hands.

Outside in the lobby I was putting my cigarettes away when I found the application form from the university folded up in my inside pocket. I sat down and scanned through it, coming to the section on fees. The first question alone, 'Please indicate how you will fund the course', was enough to burst my bubble. I tossed it in a rubbish bin on the way out.

5

I was sitting with Youssef on the cool floor of the corridor outside the children's ward. His unused crutches were by his side. Eli was standing at the other end of the corridor, our view of her occasionally blocked by passing patients and staff.

'There's a camera crew that maybe wants to do a story about you. Maybe take you to England for treatment,' I said to Youssef in Arabic. A glance at his face showed that he was having trouble understanding what I was saying. 'Do you want to do it?' My behind provided no cushion against the hard floor. He was busy picking his nose, fished something out and flicked it away.

'Will you come too?' he asked.

I wasn't expecting this question; the idea hadn't crossed my mind.

'I don't think they will pay for me to go,' I said, but my head was now full of pictures of Youssef, Eli and I spending time in London together. I saw Youssef recuperating in hospital after surgery, Eli and I going to the cinema, a restaurant, then back to the shared hotel room. My daydream was broken by its leading lady standing above me.

'I can't wait all afternoon, you know,' she said, affecting an annoyed look, her hands on her hips.

I stood up. 'OK, come on Youssef, how many times do we have to do this?' I was eager for progress with this, with something, anything.

Youssef scrunched his face angrily. 'Fuck you, you think I'm going to do this just so you can impress your girlfriend? Fuck her, and fuck your mother,' he said.

'Shut up,' I said. I picked up the crutches in one hand and tried to lift Youssef up with the other. 'Come on, try and walk.'

Eli was protesting, telling me to go easy.

'You want him to walk or not?' I said, looking her in the eye. She pulled her face back from mine. Not waiting for an answer, I forced the crutches under Youssef's arms. Youssef was muttering crude profanities just loud enough for me to hear, cataloguing the genital attributes of the females in my family, starting with my paternal grandmother and moving down the generations.

'I don't have a sister,' I said when he had finished.

'Get your hands off me,' he shouted with sudden force, his eyes shining. I looked up to see that people were becoming curious as I tried to manhandle Youssef into walking. The last thing I wanted was the daunting presence of the hospital administrator.

'I can do it alone,' Youssef hissed, trying to shrug me off with his bony shoulders.

I let go and watched him stand upright on the crutches. Eli was beside him, showing him how to take the weight on one crutch while moving the opposite leg. She stood close to him as he took a first tentative step before collapsing to the floor, his face twisted in agony, hamming it up. Eli was trying to help him up but he wouldn't let her. He looked at me, grabbing his bad leg for good measure. Eli looked at me, palms up, shrugging. If she hadn't been there maybe I would have walked right past the little bastard. As it was, I felt something for him that I couldn't explain. None of this was his fault. I lifted him from the floor and he put his skeletal arm round my neck. I carried him back to his bed, ignoring his triumphant smile.

'I'm not sure I approve of this method of physiotherapy,' Eli said later, holding my gaze.

I was the first to break eye contact. 'I'm sorry, I just got impatient.'

'Maybe you should get impatient more often.' She smiled and dug my ribs with her elbow.

'Would you like to go for a walk this evening on the seafront?' I said quickly, heart pounding and face heating up. 'I mean with me, obviously, but meet at my house ...'

'Yes, I'd like that.' Her eyes widened and she smiled. 'That would be nice.'

I bumped into Asha on the way down to the lobby. She touched my arm to stop me. It was the first time I'd seen her since that afternoon in my bedroom. She looked better now.

'I've been looking for you, are you free?'

'What do you need?' I said.

'I need your help in Intensive Care.'

As we were about to enter the unit she stopped me, saying, 'It's a burns case.'

My heart sank. I could stomach most things, but not burns. After my first time in a burns unit I'd thought about not coming back to the hospital. Traumatic amputations, disembowelments, brain-exposing head injuries, uncontrollable bleeding, facial mutilations, exposed bone and internal organs, all these I'd come to expect as the downside of living in Beirut. What I had trouble stomaching were serious burns that turned the victims into something inhuman, into writhing black and red slabs of meat. Phosphorus was the flammable material of choice that summer, the napalm of the eighties. The stuff just could not be extinguished. The burns victim would often smoke for hours. It made short work of flesh and had to be scraped off with the skin to prevent further damage. Asha knew of this weakness of mine and, after the results of my first experience, we had an unspoken agreement that I wouldn't be asked to deal with these cases. Not many serious burns victims were in a state to communicate anyway, and relatives could be talked to outside the ward, where the patient couldn't hear the bad news. I felt she should be cutting me some slack after what had happened between us. But as I followed her onto the unit I knew that nothing would get in the way of her work – not her feelings, not mine. Maybe it was a Christian thing, not that she talked of her faith, despite coming here as part of a Christian charity. As we approached the bed I kept repeating to myself, 'You're not the one who's burnt, you're not the one who's burnt,' hoping this mantra would get me beyond my revulsion. Asha pulled back a makeshift curtain: the patient was connected to a hissing respirator and thankfully covered in yellowed gauze. What must have been his extended family was around him, occupying the beds either side. Asha greeted them each by name. A young woman was dabbing the blackened forehead on the pillow with a damp cloth.

'Sharif has been kept alive on the respirator for two weeks now,' Asha said, pausing for me to translate. 'Without the respirator he cannot breathe and tests show that he will not recover.' Another pause. 'We want to ask your permission to switch off the respirator, so that Sharif can die peacefully.'

I picked my words carefully, bracing myself for an emotional response. But there was silence. The young woman turned away from me, her tears dripping onto Sharif's face. An elderly woman, whom I took to be Sharif's mother, clenched her hands together and slowly started to beat her chest, swaying back and forth. I watched as she added a slow side-to-side head movement to this assembly.

'They don't need to give us an answer now,' Asha said to me softly. 'We'll come and see them in a couple of days.'

Later that evening I was walking with Eli along the Corniche, a wide and popular promenade that had recovered its pre-war crowd. We weren't alone. John, Samir, Liv the Trotskyist and a Palestinian friend of Samir called Faris were also there. Faris was quiet, bony and tall. He had long lashes and big dark eyes, the kind that Western women always seemed to look into with tilted heads and soft faces. They'd all turned up at the same time at my flat. Samir had made much of the small spread of delicatessen goodies I'd arranged neatly on the coffee table, and had noticed that the flat had been cleaned.

'I think Ivan is expecting a woman,' he said, seemingly oblivious to my embarrassment. (I'd secretly wished for an air strike.) The bastard was still teasing me an hour later as we bought coffee from an old man with an urn on his back.

'Maybe it's that translator,' he said, flashing his inane grin at me. 'Hey, Eli, do you think she and Ivan would be good together?'

'They're well suited, I'm sure,' said Eli, who had kept quiet on arriving at the flat, although I thought I caught a fleeting expression of regret around her mouth, a slight pinking of her cheeks when she saw the food and the two wine glasses. Thinking about it again made me cringe. We were overtaken by a group of teenage boys wearing their best clothes and stinking of aftershave. They paraded past a group of made-up girls. Glances were exchanged as the two groups passed, and a person broke away from each group to chat briefly before running to catch up with their friends. We walked over to the waist-high railing that looked out to sea. The tide was out and three men were down on the rocky seashore, firing an automatic rifle at a distant floating barrel. We stopped to watch. One of them noticed that there were foreigners leaning over the railing.

'Hello, you shoot?' one of them shouted in English, laughing with the others at the idea. John climbed over the railing and slid down the wall onto the rocky shore. Samir followed, shouting for him to wait. We watched as John took the weapon, expertly loading a round into the breech even as the man was asking whether John knew what to do. He rested on one knee and took aim through his glasses. He looked as if he was ignoring the advice of the men whose gun he was about to fire. Releasing the safety he single-fired at the barrel, a shot a second, creating a splash of sea water around it then successive clanking pops as he punctured the metal. There was a smattering of applause as he handed the weapon back. He made his way back to the railing, grinning, followed by Samir. Faris and I helped them scramble up the wall. We walked on.

'Where does a doctor learn to shoot like that?' asked Faris, obviously impressed.

'British army, Black Watch regiment, medical corps. The SLR they have down there is standard issue.'

'Maybe they got it from an English peacekeeping soldier,' Faris said. 'I hear you can buy weapons from some of the foreign soldiers.'

'Wouldn't have got it from a Scottish one, that's for sure,' said John. He smiled but I could tell he meant it.

I wanted to ask him about being in the army, but two cars were approaching fast down the Corniche, Lebanese flags flying from windows plastered with pictures of Bashir Gemayel. Just as they passed us they were brought to a squealing halt by someone pulling out in front of them. The drivers pressed on their horns.

'Who's the man on the poster?' asked Eli. 'His face is everywhere.'

'He's going to be the new president,' Liv answered. 'He's a Phalange, a right-wing Christian. He hates the Palestinians, wants to expel them from Lebanon. He cooperated with the Israelis during the invasion of his own country.'

Faris raised his black eyebrows, looking down his long nose at Liv.

'You have a good knowledge of Lebanese politics,' he said.

'You're surprised because I am a woman,' she said, tilting her head at him.

He laughed, revealing a gold tooth. 'No, because you are a foreigner,' he said.

I heard shouting behind us; the driver of the car that had pulled out was on the street, gesticulating at the two honking cars, whose occupants stayed put.

'We're not all ignorant,' Liv said.

There was a pop. The shouting driver was silenced; he disappeared from view. There were screams from people on the pavement.

'We need to move,' said Faris. He was herding us into a tight group, looking around him. The screams were replaced by rapid gunfire from the shore side of the promenade. We all crouched instinctively. People were running towards us. I turned to see the barrel shooters firing at the poster-covered cars through the railings. We were close enough to see the spent cartridges spinning on the pavement. Faris signalled for us to follow him as car doors started to open. He led us away from the crowd, running across the road hunched down. I looked round to see several men get out of the two cars and start to return fire into the railings. Faris led us up an alley where we slowed to a walk, too breathless to speak. Samir and I were bent over, trying to take in air. Samir took out a packet of Marlboro and offered me one. I waved it away in disgust.

'Who were they, the men on the beach?' asked Eli. She was still finding her breath, leaning on Liv for support.

'Cowboys,' said Faris. 'The same guys who were driving around

Hamra in jeeps during the siege but never saw the frontline. Stupid
fucking cowboys.'

'I need a drink,' said Liv.

Back at the flat we drank warm Stolichnaya and ate my salami and
olives. John put on a Donovan record. Although we had electricity,
the preference was for candles. To me, the orange light made everyone
look haggard and ill. I felt a certain detachment, as if I was behind
a screen of frosted glass. I became intrigued by a delay between
people's mouths moving and the sound reaching my ears, like a
badly dubbed film. Faris and Liv were arguing, something about
the permanent revolution and the failings of the Arab bourgeoisie.
Donovan was singing about someone being a Catholic as well as a
Hindu, an atheist and a Jew. Someone was explaining the falling out
of Trotsky and Lenin and the use of icepicks. Samir was telling Liv
that women shouldn't be so serious. Liv was telling him that perhaps
men should be more serious. My hands were clammy, I wanted to
wipe them on my shirt but they wouldn't move, they were stuck to
my thighs. I wanted to tell people this; it was interesting and they
needed to know. Someone was asking me a question but I couldn't
make out the words or who was saying them. Whoever it was got
up slowly; perhaps I'd made them angry and they were coming over
to confront me? John loomed into focus. I tried to tell him that
he was in focus; he would be pleased at this news. Something was
hovering just beyond my mental grasp, something important that
I felt I must share once I got hold of it. I saw a flash of light, then
everything went dark.

I opened my eyes to see Eli and John looking down at me. I
felt the rug beneath my back, saw the shadows on the living-room
ceiling. One of them was holding my wrist while the other was
wiping my forehead.

'Bach or Mozart?' asked John.

'Er ... Bach,' I said.

'Good lad. How do you feel?'

'Tired.'

'You've had an epileptic fit, laddie.' He was smiling. 'Too much vodka, too little food.' He wiped some saliva from my chin. I looked at Eli. I could now tell that it was her hand on my brow.

'When you're ready,' John said, putting a hand under my shoulder. They walked me to the bedroom despite my protests. I lay on the bed.

'You should rest,' John said.

'I'll stay with him for a few minutes,' Eli told John.

'The nurse will take over,' John said to me. He turned to Eli. 'He needs to sleep though.'

She frowned at him, pointing to the door. He left and she knelt down and removed my trainers, jeans and shirt. This was the stuff of fantasies but I felt drained and, besides, she did it with such reassuring, professional movements that I was completely at ease. The fit had left me feeling mellow, floating. She pulled the sheet and blanket over me and sat on the side of the bed.

'You should look after yourself better.' She said this matter-of-factly, putting a hand to my forehead. I closed my eyes as she stroked my brow. I could hear the others talking, their voices a soothing mumble in the background. The last thing I remembered was the door closing then some rustling, like someone getting undressed.

6

I woke to find Eli beside me in bed, her face towards mine, eyes closed. I didn't move, watching her breathe softly, her lips slightly parted, some dried saliva at the corner of her mouth. Her hand was on the pillow by her face: I saw the wedding ring she no longer needed but wore because she'd been told it was better, as a foreign woman, to appear married in a place like Beirut. It bit into her finger. Her bra strap, visible where the blanket had slipped, bit into her shoulder. It was the first time I'd spent the night with a woman, yet nothing had happened. My mouth was dry so I slipped out of bed and put on my jeans.

Liv was standing naked in front of the open fridge.

'How are you this morning?' she asked, putting her hand to my cheek. She looked concerned. 'We were worried. That was an impressive epileptic fit.'

I told her I was fine, keeping my eyes fixed on hers. I found a clean glass and tried the tap. Luck was on my side and I gulped voraciously, trying not to think of the rusting tank the water sat in on the roof. Liv headed back to her room with a plate of leftover salami; I watched her walk down the corridor. John was under a blanket on the sofa in the living room. Without waking him I opened the balcony door to release the stale smell of tobacco. I could hear

Faris's muffled deep tones and Liv's laughter through their bedroom wall. Eli was dressing when I went back into my room.

'Are you going?' I asked, not hiding the disappointment in my voice.

'Don't look so sad,' she said. 'I have to get my things from the hotel.'

'Your things?' Surely she wasn't planning to bring her stuff back here?

'Before I go to work of course.'

Of course, how stupid of me. My gaze went to her hips; dark hair had escaped from under the top of her white underwear. She pulled on her jeans and looked at me as she tied her hair into two pigtails, finishing them off with black ribbons. I could see her as a girl, with her hair done in the same way.

'I'm sorry about yesterday, I couldn't stop the others coming too,' she said, stepping forward. She kissed me briefly on the lips, her hands cool on my bare shoulders. In the hallway she stopped with the front door open. 'Have some breakfast. I'll come by and cook something tonight.'

I picked a spare key from a hook by the door and handed it to her.

'In case you get back before me,' I said.

'I guess this means things are serious between us,' she said, raising her eyebrows at me to show she was joking.

I had no time for breakfast. I was supposed to meet Najwa and I didn't want to be late. When I turned into Rue Descartes I was surprised to see her walking towards me, her limp less evident than usual. I knew I was early and wanted to say so but remembered the rule about not recognising each other in public. I glanced at her as we passed and she shook her head slightly, a warning in her eyes. Not wanting to abruptly stop and turn around behind her, I continued walking. As I approached the entrance to the apartment block I saw what had spooked Najwa: the black Mercedes parked outside, the smoking driver leaning against it, not bothering to hide the automatic protruding from his belt. He turned to look at me through sunglasses too big for his face. Without slowing down I passed the entrance, looking inside and taking in the two men talking to the old lady who had questioned my presence in the hall. Luckily she didn't see me and I resisted the urge to sprint round the corner.

Ten minutes later I found myself outside the Commodore Hotel and went in on a whim, thinking it was a safe place to be for a while. Reporters were sitting in the lobby, waiting for something to happen. The war was finished for them; just the US marines' departure in a few days and then home. I sat down and picked up an *International Herald Tribune*. The headline read 'ARAB LEADERS DISCUSS MIDEAST PEACE STRATEGY'. I was wondering whether I should go back to Najwa's apartment when a finger appeared over my shoulder, jabbing at the headline.

'A complete waste of time. It will amount to nothing,' Samir said. 'Come on. Bob wants to go to the Green Line.'

The Green Line, demarcation between west and east, Christian and Muslim, Left and Right. It wasn't that simple (there were many Christians in west Beirut) and yet this shorthand served a purpose, making it easier to digest the unpalatable reality of the city. The old city centre was badly scarred, not from the invasion this summer but from the Civil War. Left-wing militias were handing over token weapons to the Lebanese army and giving up long-held positions. This was the ideal opportunity to illustrate Bob's story on the return to normality in what he called (off camera) the 'asshole' of the world.

After filming pockmarked buildings and the burnt-out Holiday Inn, used as a vantage point for snipers, Bob wanted to go to the east.

'I know a great fish restaurant there,' he said.

'I don't know. I should really get back,' I said.

'It's just across the line, ten minutes at most.'

I looked at Samir who shrugged and looked away. 'He's the boss,' he said in Arabic.

The crossing was uneventful. We passed unchallenged through a Lebanese army checkpoint and drove through streets like the ones we'd left behind, although there was less evidence of bomb damage. The restaurant was full of people: families, couples and a group of loud young men. We attracted attention, as Bob didn't want to leave his huge Sony video camera in the car. A round-bellied man approached us, grinning, arms outstretched.

'Hello, Mr Bob. Welcome. We have not seen you for some time.'

'Small matter of a siege, Mr Khoury,' Bob said, which caused the fat man to guffaw. He showed us to a table overlooking the shore.

Bob wolfed his grilled fish, easing it down with cold Heineken. I picked at mine. My buttocks clenched as I noticed one of the young men get up from his table and approach ours. I had trouble swallowing. He stood at our table.

'Television?' he asked in English, pointing at the camera, microphone and video pack.

Bob nodded, his mouth full of tomato salad.

'And you guys, where are you from?' the man asked, this time in Arabic, looking at Samir and me.

'From Beirut,' said Samir, smiling.

'East or west?' came back the question unsmilingly.

I felt for my passport, made eyes at Bob.

'There is no more east or west, my friend,' said Samir.

I wondered where he got his cool. The man looked back at his friends.

'We need to make tracks,' I said quietly to Bob, hoping that this was an American expression. Another man had detached himself from the group; now they were all staring over at our table. Barrel-chested and with a shaved head, he was putting on dark glasses as he approached us.

Bob took a swig of beer and stood up, picking up the camera.

'You good-looking guys want to be on TV?' he said to the men. They both grinned and Bob winked at me. 'It works every time,' he said.

Back through the Green Line, I started to breathe again.

'When did you last go to east Beirut?' Bob asked when Samir stopped to drop me off.

'Never,' I told him.

It was getting dark on Najwa's balcony. I sucked in cigarette smoke like it had life-enhancing properties.

'Turns out Nabil is an Israeli informer,' Najwa said.

'Nabil?'

'The guy you exchanged envelopes with at the university.'

'Shit.' I inhaled more smoke, looking out at the lights in east Beirut; west Beirut was in darkness. I imagined Nabil over there, laughing at us over here suckered into a summer of solidarity with him. He was probably eating fish in the very restaurant I'd lunched at that day, giving my description to a Mossad officer. 'Are you telling us, Nabil dear friend, that this is the best you can come up with?' Of course they'd probably taken photographs.

'Does he know where you live?' asked Najwa, gulping red wine like it was iced water.

'No, we only met at the university.'

We both looked questioningly at each other, thinking back to any contacts we had had with Nabil. It occurred to me that Nabil might know where Najwa lived, but surely we wouldn't have been sitting in her apartment if that was the case. I kept a nervous eye on the front door anyway.

'In that case we might have to use your apartment. If it isn't compromised, that is. We'll give it a few days to make sure.'

'Use it for what?' I asked, thinking maybe they needed to store things in it, documents or forging equipment.

'Nabil knew where one of our cadres was staying. He moved as soon as we realised what had happened but he can't stay where he is for long. Your place isn't known to anyone.'

I nodded, not wanting to speak in case I betrayed my reluctance. It meant the end of waking up to Eli in my bed. I wished I'd been conscious to see her get into it.

'Are you going to be alright with this, Ivan?'

'Yes. Yes of course.'

'What about Samir, do you still see him?'

'I bump into him occasionally. He's harmless.'

She didn't look convinced. 'OK. Listen. There's going to be a meeting of cadres in a few days. I need you to watch the place where the meeting happens. Look out for anything suspicious.' Najwa refilled my glass then her own.

'Is a meeting a good idea? I mean, getting all those people together in one place,' I asked. Maybe I was just fearful about being in close proximity to such a gathering given the news about Lazy Eye, or maybe I was just curious, but judging by the look Najwa gave me I seemed to have forgotten my place.

'Just come back in a couple of days, Ivan.'

I was surprised to find my apartment full of people, but then I remembered I'd given Eli a key that morning. Asha, John, Eli, Faris, Samir and Liv were there, as well as some others I didn't know. Joan Baez was on the turntable. The smell of hashish came from the living room, the smell of frying garlic from the kitchen. I followed the garlic. Asha, shaking a frying pan over a flame, gave me a one-armed hug and a professional once-over.

'I heard about your petit mal,' she said. Chicken joints lay on the side; Samir was finely chopping a huge bunch of parsley to go into his salad.

'This recipe has been handed down from generation to generation in my family,' he told Eli, winking at me.

We sat around the coffee table in the living room after dinner. Asha passed a joint from Samir to Liv without it touching her lips.

John, exclaiming that he'd nearly forgotten, handed me a plastic bag. Inside were little square bars, each in a white cellophane wrapping. John took one out and held it up between his fingers.

'Red Cross survival bars: one of these a day will satisfy all your daily nutrient requirements,' he said in a cheesy American voice, like in a TV advert. The joint came back to him. 'Wherever there is war, famine or disease, all you need is one of these to forget your woes. Poverty doesn't matter any more with the Red Cross nutrient bar, designed to counter even the most deprived diet. Unable to prepare a meal due to bombing and shelling? Then the Red Cross nutrient bar is the answer.' He recovered his normal voice, 'Anyway laddie, make sure you have one of these for breakfast every day.'

Samir was constructing a new joint by rolling the tobacco out of a Marlboro without breaking the paper, mixing it with hashish and funnelling it back into the empty casing.

'How long have you known Samir?' Eli asked me. She was sitting back in the sofa, her legs tucked beneath her.

'A few months,' I told her. 'He saved me from a wild dog.'

Samir laughed more loudly than usual. 'A wild dog on a football pitch,' he said in a constricted voice, trying to keep the smoke in his lungs.

'A football pitch full of cars,' I said, giggling – I wasn't sure how I could be smoking the joint at the same time as Samir.

'It was the middle of the night,' said Samir, starting to giggle as well.

'OK. I'm curious,' said Liv.

I competed with Samir to see who could stop giggling first. John put Nina Simone on. I was deciding how to tell the story without giving too much away; a part of my brain still retained some caution.

'Well, to cut a long story short – I was on the football pitch in Fakhani, this was some time in July. It was the middle of the night but there was a full moon.' I took a drink of Stolichnaya, now mixed with long-life orange juice for health reasons. 'A lot of people had parked their cars on the pitch. They thought it was safer than leaving them in the streets under the apartment blocks, you know, to stop the rubble falling on them. Anyway, most people seemed to have left them there when they moved to safer areas.'

'But what were you doing there?' asked Liv.

'Siphoning petrol from the parked cars. Generators were the only source of electricity and we'd run out of fuel.' The Lebanese Gold and Stolichnaya had weakened my inhibition and I struggled to avoid telling them why we needed to run generators in Fakhani in the middle of the war. A part of me wanted to tell them everything, to be completely open. Najwa would have killed me.

'Anyway, a pack of abandoned dogs was roaming around the

stadium, maybe ten of them, you know, looking for scraps to eat. I could see them circling as I tried to suck petrol from the tanks. Then the shelling starts. One of the shells falls quite close, on the pitch, and I can hear the dogs howling, like they're scared.' I sipped my drink, passed the joint to Eli.

'I see one of the dogs approaching. It's limping. It's lost one of its legs in the explosion so it's confused and in pain. It thinks I caused its injury so it starts barking at me, baring its teeth, frothing at the mouth. But I can't go anywhere because of the shelling. I'm pinned against the cars.' I paused and Samir took up the story.

'I was working in Fakhani, waiting in my car on the street.' Probably waiting for my father, I thought. 'When the bombs came down I went inside to the pitch, because I thought it would be safer in there, I don't like to be inside a building in case it falls down on your head. I saw Ivan hiding by a car with a can of petrol and the dog with three legs coming towards him. It looked crazy, this dog.'

'What did you do?' asked Eli.

He took sight down an imaginary rifle. 'I shot it.' There were a few seconds' silence.

'The start of a beautiful friendship,' said John.

Samir and I started giggling again but I saw that no one else was laughing except Faris, who was just smiling to himself. I tried to stop. I caught Eli giving me a look. She put a hand on my arm, as if to calm me down.

In truth I knew little about Samir. We'd met when he started driving my father around just before the invasion and had continued throughout the siege. He was a friend forged from adversity. We were very different. Samir was uneducated and, apart from running his little café, drove for a living. He had moved around the different factions of the PLO and Lebanese Left depending on which one he got on with or paid better. I, on the other hand, had gone with my father's organisation, done the training, and joined Signals without giving much thought to the politics or whether I agreed with them. In a sense I was no better than my old schoolmates Bedrosian and Mustapha, joining their fathers' import-export businesses, except that they would probably make good businessmen, whereas I knew that I would never be the politician my father was.

Samir took another drag on his re-engineered Marlboro then examined the end.

'This was grown here in Lebanon,' he said to nobody in particular.

'Probably the best export Lebanon has to offer,' said John.

Later in bed I struggled with my disappointment at Eli not staying the night, although I hadn't dared ask her in front of the others. Instead I was stuck with Samir in the other bedroom and John on the sofa. I told myself that she was too old for me, that she had a child not much younger than Youssef, that she had a partner waiting in Norway. I told myself these things but they didn't help me sleep. I replaced them with thoughts of waking up beside her and her goodbye kiss before she went to work, her hands on my shoulders. Except the way I remembered it she hadn't got dressed and was pulling me back to bed.

7

Donkey Man was up and walking on crutches, visiting all the patients on his floor as part of what he was calling his 'daily routine', even though it was only day one. Eli said it was excellent physiotherapy. He'd also been discovered by distant relatives, who came across him while visiting someone in the same ward. Eli and I were now sitting in their two-room breeze-block home as they'd insisted she come for tea. I hadn't been invited but Eli had asked me along to translate and chaperone. But I was happy to be here, pretending we were a couple. Sweet, strong tea was served in small glasses. We were offered food: cakes and sweets, their syrupy glaze glistening in what little light filtered through the single window. Eli ate out of politeness; I'd told her it was rude to decline these offerings. I nibbled at a sweet pastry, embarrassed at how much effort they'd gone to, given their circumstances. An elderly woman showed Eli her embroidery: intricate, colourful needlework covering every inch of a shawl. I was translating for her, explaining to Eli that the patterns differed according to which area you came from back home. Back home was Palestine, which the woman hadn't seen for thirty-odd years, not since the Naqba, which I translated as 'the catastrophe'. Her pride in her work reminded me of my Danish grandmother's complex Hedebo embroidery. I could picture both women exchanging stitching tips. Neighbours arrived to have a look at Eli, and I was starting to tire from the introductions and from having to say my name at least twice to every person.

I thought, not for the first time, how something as simple as a name could set you apart, particularly in Lebanon. To have a name clearly defining one side or the other, though making life easier in some respects, could have been worse, as it would have pigeonholed me, and the truth was I didn't feel one thing or the other. Maybe, I thought, sucking half-dissolved sugar from the bottom of my glass, I had the perfect name. Maybe it wasn't my problem at all, but everybody else's. I was interrupted by Eli tugging at my sleeve, telling me she had to get back to work.

At the hospital the English film crew was on the kids' ward filming the photogenic girl having her prosthetic refitted. There were more medics around the bed than the girl had ever seen, even when she came in with her leg dangling by cartilage several weeks before. Youssef was heckling in English from his bed.

'Have my picture! I can speak the English. I love England. I love Manchester United.' He sniggered as the girl tried to walk with the prosthetic.

I told him to shut up, asked him whether he was going to try walking himself rather than just mocking others.

'I have nowhere to go,' he said. 'Anyway, I prefer the wheelchair.' He'd discovered that he could shoot around in a wheelchair, terrorising those who couldn't move as quickly.

'You need to exercise your legs. Eli will be angry with you,' I said.

The cameraman rearranged people around the girl's bed.

'Eli is going home soon. Anyway, she doesn't get angry.' Youssef started to throw roasted nuts at the gathering around the girl's bed, making bomb-falling noises to accompany their flight. One landed on the producer's head.

'What do you mean?' I asked, taking the bag of nuts from him. 'She's never angry, she's too soft.'

'No, not that – what do you mean she's leaving soon?'

Youssef's face lit up. 'You don't know that your girlfriend is leaving,' he said in an annoying sing-song voice.

I could feel my ears get hot. 'She's not my girlfriend,' I said, loud enough for the soundman to look round angrily and ask for yet another take.

I found Eli with Samir in the lobby. She was laughing at some joke of his a little too enthusiastically.

'You want a lift back to town?' Samir asked me. I told him I'd meet him outside but he stayed where he was.

'I need to speak to her alone,' I told him in Arabic.

'OK, I understand,' he said in English, winking and grinning at Eli.

'What was that about?' asked Eli, pointing at Samir's back.

'Is it true you're leaving soon? When are you leaving? You didn't tell me you were leaving.'

She put up her hands to shield herself from my barrage. 'Relax. Did you think I was staying for ever?' Her voice was low, her tone even, and this calmed me down, made me realise that I was being unreasonable.

'I'm sorry. I didn't ask when you were going home before. I forget that you have a life waiting for you outside this,' I said, gesturing at the lobby. She nodded. There seemed to be more women and children camped in the lobby than before. I couldn't understand why they were here.

'I'm due to leave on the fifteenth. I've been trying not to think about it.' She pulled at her obsolete wedding ring. 'It will be difficult to go.' I studied a small blemish on her right iris. She looked at me with questioning eyes. I wanted to kiss her; instead I stuffed my hands deep into my pockets. Despite myself, I was leaning towards her. Eli looked at me with concern, pulling back.

'Let's talk later,' she said, looking around, worried about how this would look. I was behaving like the teenager I was. I heard a siren outside, a screeching of tyres then screaming and shouting. These were not good sounds. Four men, one of them Samir, were rushing into the lobby with a stretcher. A shrieking teenage boy was on it, his right leg ending below the knee in a stub of bone and blackened flesh. His left leg was intact but a bloody pulp. A group of people followed the stretcher, their shouting and wailing competing with the boy's screams. Asha had appeared from nowhere, dragging me into the emergency room.

'Ivan, tell the boy to keep still. Hold him still,' Asha ordered. She told Samir to remove everyone who didn't need to be there. He herded the family outside. His presence was helpful; they took him more seriously than they would me. As I was trying to calm the boy down the film crew, attracted by the tell-tale sounds of decent footage, had found their way into the emergency room, now filled only with the sound of the screaming boy. Asha released a makeshift tourniquet from above his right knee and blood shot from the stump. She tried to find the offending artery and clamp it. The producer looked away, her face white and clammy. A Palestinian doctor was trying to inject painkiller into his arm but the boy was flailing and trying to sit up to look at his legs. Samir helped me hold him down while a nurse tried to find a vein to fill him with morphine.

'We'll have to remove this one,' Asha said, as if talking about an offending hangnail, holding up the frayed left leg which was attached by only skin and flesh to the knee. The cameraman had zoomed in at this point, filling his viewfinder with gore. He lowered the camera. There were tears streaking his cheeks.

'I can't do this,' he said to no one in particular, turning away.

The doctors were oblivious to him as they prepared the now zombified boy for surgery, wheeling him through the double doors, leaving silence in the air and blood on the floor behind them.

After telling the boy's relatives what was going on, I sat in Samir's latest mode of transport, a Nissan Patrol with black UN markings on the sides, standard United Nations war-zone issue. Ordinarily I would have been curious as to how Samir got hold of the vehicle but I was reliving my aborted conversation with Eli, unhappy at the way it ended, embarrassed about my behaviour. John and Liv were also in the car and I agreed to go for a drink with them at the Etoile, where most of the volunteers were posted. John himself was posted in a smaller hotel, since he hadn't come with the same charity as the Scandinavians or Asha. He was telling me that Asha was moving out of the Etoile, which she hated, to stay on the AUB campus in an apartment belonging to a literature professor who had left for America in July.

'It's on the seventh floor and looks over the sea,' John was saying. 'We should visit her when she moves in, sit on her balcony and read books. Asha says the place is full of books. I miss books.'

I used to read a lot to escape the Danish-Palestinian war that was home, taking refuge under a large pair of headphones to muffle the vocal nature of the conflict. It was a war that had started in 1979, after my brother Karam died falling six floors from a balcony. When he'd fallen he'd broken the family, not just his body. It wasn't a thing that could be fixed, despite my parents' efforts. Karam had been as dark as Youssef, taking after my father in looks, whereas I was tempered by my mother's Nordic genes. Consequently Karam had always been accepted as more of an Arab than I was. I suspected my father preferred Karam for that reason.

I tried to picture the walls of books in our old apartment, the one we were in before we had to move to the relative safety of where I was now staying. Over the last few months the desire to open a book had dissipated, their imagined worlds paling in contrast to the daily excitement of reality. I made a mental note to visit the old apartment as I'd promised my parents, to make sure that all our things were still there.

The combination of the UN jeep and white-skinned passengers meant we were waved through a Lebanese army roadblock unchecked. All of us, apart from Samir, avoided the volunteers congregated in the bar of the hotel and headed for Liv's room. We found the anaesthetist asleep on Liv's bed underneath a Scandinavian airline poster of a fjord; she was one of Liv's four roommates. She'd been on night duty. I was surprised to see Faris asleep in one of the other beds. Liv slapped him on the behind, causing him to sit bolt upright with a terrified look on his face.

'Poor guy probably thought they'd come to get him,' said John, pouring Johnny Walker into plastic cups. Faris forced a smile. Liv apologised, offering an embarrassed grin and ruffling his already unkempt hair. I could see an old bullet scar under his right clavicle and wondered what the exit wound looked like the other side. Liv stripped to her underwear and got into bed with him. I removed my sneakers and lay on Eli's empty bed, resting my drink on my chest. I studied a picture of Eli's son on the bedside table, looking for a likeness, trying to remember what he was called. John was perched on the fourth bed; he removed his glasses and rubbed his eyes. No one spoke. We drank our whisky and listened to the anaesthetist's quiet snoring.

Later that night Faris, Liv and I walked through the cooled streets towards my apartment. Samir had gone to pick up the late shift from Sabra, filling the Nissan with nervous-looking young foreign women for the night shift and shouting in Arabic (thankfully) as he left, 'I may just go straight home with this lot.' John had gone back to his billet, pleading exhaustion. The streets were darkened by a power cut and lack of moon; no light came from the buildings, not even the orange glow of a candle. There was an unspoken need to stay silent, and Liv whispered to ask me again whether it was OK for them to stay with me. I told her that I couldn't be happier, that I didn't want to be alone. To my embarrassment and Faris's amusement, she stopped to give me a hug.

'We would never leave you alone, would we Faris?'

I could smell the Johnny Walker on her breath as I returned her hug, pretending to sob.

Faris laughed and patted me on the back. 'You are like our little brother,' he said.

Back at the apartment they retreated to the spare bedroom, leaving me with the candle-lit vista of the bottle-strewn coffee table, the bottles' shadows shifting together in response to the dancing flame. I watched candle wax drip down my Chianti bottle, the new soft wax finding the easiest route over the old hard wax, slowing down as it hardened. I found some music to put on, just to drown out the sound of Liv's grunting from the next room, but remembered that the power was cut. Liv went silent and I heard a quiet knock at the door.

I could see Eli smiling through the peephole, her face distorted by the small convex lens. I smiled then realised that she couldn't see me.

We sat together on the sofa, shoulders touching, feet on the table. I had poured her some wine; she rested the glass on her lap.

'That boy who came in today, he didn't live through the surgery,' she said. 'Asha said he'd already lost too much blood when he arrived at the hospital.'

I caught myself before I said anything trite, preferring to remain silent. I was sick of platitudes, sick of having to hand them out to relatives.

'What is the worst thing that has happened to you in this war?' she asked. 'Was it the dog in the stadium? You don't have to tell me,' she added quickly.

I knew what I wanted to tell her. I wanted to tell her how I'd seen Karam run onto the balcony of a friend's apartment and just keep going, tumbling over the railing, his little hand momentarily grabbing for the rail. I wanted to but I couldn't. Instead I remembered something else I hadn't told anyone.

'It was during the Civil War in the seventies. When the shelling was bad from the east we used to take shelter in the hall of the apartment. It was in the middle and had only one small window, which faced away from east Beirut. It was the safest place to be.' I leant forward and picked at the rim of the candle on the Chianti bottle to let more wax flow out, trying to direct it towards an exposed bit of glass. 'We'd gone there one night when they were falling a little close. It seemed to go on for hours. It's difficult to explain how loud shelling is. It overwhelms everything, drives the very thoughts from your head. When it stopped it was so quiet.' I took a sip of wine from Eli's glass. 'That's when it started. The screaming. We could hear it through the window, someone in the street. Horrible screaming, you could tell it was a man in terrible pain. I'd never heard a man scream before. The thing is, it went on for what seemed like ages – it wouldn't stop. It was worse than the shelling. Putting your hands over your ears didn't help. I just wanted him to stop.' I looked into the candle flame. 'I wanted him to die. It's terrible to say but I just wanted the screaming to stop.'

'What happened?' Eli asked, recovering her glass from my hand, letting her fingers linger on mine.

'The shelling started again. They often did that – stopped shelling until people went out to recover the wounded or check the damage, then they'd start again. Anyway, when it eventually stopped he stopped screaming. Turned out it was the man who owned the corner shop.'

We were both holding the stem of the glass, would probably be holding hands if the glass weren't there.

'It's OK,' she said, squeezing my hand, 'you were just a kid. Kids aren't supposed to hear things like that.'

I could feel my throat constrict with mawkish self-pity at her kindness. I strangled it with a question. 'What made you decide to come here, to Beirut?'

'I wish I could say it was for a noble reason,' she said. 'The truth is it was convenient for me to be here. I was, I am still, going through a difficult time with my partner in Norway and we needed to spend time apart. Liv was planning to come here; we work at the same hospital in Oslo, you see. She always supports different causes, she's a good person like that. I decided at the last minute to come with her, even though I knew nothing about the situation; just what I saw on the TV.' We watched the flames. 'Are you disappointed with my reason for coming?' she asked.

'No, it makes you more human. Anyway, it doesn't matter why you're here. You are making a difference. Maybe even more than someone who came here for political reasons.'

She shook her head. 'Not really,' she said, 'but it's making a difference to me.'

'And to me,' I said. I was glad she couldn't see my burning face in the inadequate light. We watched the candle some more. She felt like a radiator beside me, giving off heat.

'It's too late for me to go back to the hotel, I think,' she said.

'You can sleep here.' I patted the sofa as an afterthought.

'I can share with you in your bed – if that's OK?'

'That's OK too.'

'Just sleeping, like before.'

'Just sleeping,' I said.

I thought I'd hidden my disappointment well but she took my hand asking softly, 'If it's a problem I can stay on the sofa?'

I shook my head, not wanting to spoil the mood by talking about sex. Maybe that would come later.

8

I was sitting in a coffee bar watching the entrance to the building opposite where the cadres were meeting to discuss whatever cadres needed to discuss when in hiding. I was trying to make my coffee last as long as possible but had to leave after the waiter came up for the second time in three minutes to ask whether I wanted something else. I had no more money so I took to the street, watching, but not sure what for: suspicious cars full of men in sunglasses, jeeps full of armed troops screeching to a halt outside the entrance, someone leaving a large suitcase against the door. Najwa had given me a walkie-talkie, to be used only in an emergency. Unfortunately it was of military specification rather than one for clandestine use by agents of the state, or agents without a state – a hefty thing with a long aerial, intended for the rigours of battle. I had to put it in a carrier bag found in her kitchen when it wouldn't fit the small inside pocket of my denim jacket. If it came to it and I had to take the damn thing out I might as well jump up and down shouting, 'I'm here, come and get me!'

Half an hour and a Red Cross nutrition bar later I had exhausted my window shopping, which was limited to a handful of places, and caught the shopkeeper's eye as I stood outside an Islamic bookstore for the fifth time. The bookstore sat between a closed record shop displaying a copy of Pink Floyd's 'The Wall' in the window and the stationers where I used to get the lined notebooks specified by school.

Turning to look up the street to check the entrance to the building I was horrified to see John and Asha walking towards me. They hadn't seen me so I decided to cross the road, causing an old taxi to screech to a halt against my legs, bumper touching denim. The driver started leaning on the horn as if it would blow me out of the way and simultaneously stuck his head out of his window to let me know, in a screeching voice, how stupid I was, being descended from a donkey. Naturally enough, the commotion attracted the interest of passers-by, who initially kept a respectable distance in case weapons were drawn. I saw Asha and John waving at me, attracted by the commotion, and I stood frozen in the street as the traffic built up. An orchestra of horns had started and, realising that I was no longer holding the plastic bag, I desperately rooted around on the ground for it, retrieving it from under the front bumper of the taxi, now revving its engine ready for the Grand Prix circuit that was Beirut. Asha and John joined me on the street, John giving the taxi driver some Glaswegian invective to match his Lebanese abuse. The crowd – now that a small Indian woman and blond man had entered the fracas and no gunfight had broken out – joined in. Being a spectator was never enough in Lebanon; everyone had an opinion to give and blame to apportion. Eventually the crowd was manoeuvred to the pavement and the traffic started to move, horns blaring parting shots. People started to drift away, the entertainment now over, and I was left with John and Asha asking me what I was doing here.

'I'm just waiting to meet some old school friends,' I said, pointing to the coffee shop in the belief that its existence made my story more credible.

'We're going to Samir's restaurant for lunch, to try some of his renowned falafel,' Asha said, showing me her perfectly formed teeth.

'Obviously you haven't been there before,' I said. My eyes darted to the secret meeting location. For all I knew the cadres could have left in the commotion and I could be sitting here for hours waiting for them to come out. Worse still, an assassination team could have entered the building while I was busy being run over outside. I wished Asha and John would leave. This was an unwelcome leakage of one compartmentalised bit of my life into the other. I saw John glance at my carrier bag, a question (I was sure) starting to form on his lips.

'Ah, I can see one of my friends,' I said quickly, looking over their shoulders. 'I'd better be going. See you later?' I started to cross the road, more carefully this time, and looked back to see them watching, probably curious to see what my mysterious friends looked like. I stopped on the other side and shouted to them: 'Don't eat Samir's secret sauce.' They laughed and, to my relief, started to walk off. I went back into the coffee shop to see the same waiter standing before me, arms crossed.

'What, now you have some money?'

Having given the walkie-talkie back to Najwa and had lunch with her and drunk some coffee, she confirmed that one of the cadres would be staying with me in a couple of days. She wouldn't tell me who it was 'for my own good' and asked me whether there had been any suspicious callers or 'anything like that'. I couldn't think of anything in particular, everything looked suspicious at that point. A group of young men standing on the street made me wonder what they were up to (they were probably the same men who stood there during the siege, except now they were unarmed). Seeing two men sitting in a car made me cross the road in case they were a snatch squad. Ever since I'd heard that Nabil (or Lazy Eye, as I still thought of him) had turned out to be an informer, the whole appeal of this secret existence seemed less attractive to me. The glamour, such as it was, had gone. This wasn't John Le Carré: as I recalled, Smiley's people hadn't wandered around with huge walkie-talkies or without enough change to buy coffee.

I consoled myself on the way to Samir's falafel place with thoughts of Eli and myself in bed the night before. We had slept in our underwear, me careful to hide my arousal by moving my hips away from her as we lay 'like spoons in a drawer', as she put it. Unfortunately, every time I moved she would grind her buttocks back into my groin. Eventually I managed to make things subside by thinking of Youssef's wound being dressed and mentally stripping my Tokarev. That morning I had left her sleeping so I wouldn't have to explain where I was going. I'd found Liv naked in the kitchen again and, to her amusement, had fetched a robe for her to put on: there was only so much I could take.

Faris was with two men I hadn't seen before in Samir's café, huddled together at a back table, one that Samir saved for his 'special' customers. I noticed that the two men leant towards Faris to listen or talk to him, not the other way round. I guessed they held him in some respect. I couldn't see Samir so I walked towards Faris's table. As I approached he got up and met me half way, drawing me to the counter by the elbow. He smelt of tobacco and aftershave.

'Buy you a sandwich?' he asked with a bit too much enthusiasm, not his usual laid-back self.

I explained that I'd eaten, that I was looking for Samir.

'He's gone to the airport, some of the foreigners are leaving.'

This information filled my head with thoughts of Eli being driven to the airport. I accepted an ice-cold bottle of Coca-Cola from Faris.

'Who are your friends?' I asked, nodding towards the group at the table.

'Just some brothers from the organisation,' he said. He looked at me as if to gauge my reaction. 'We're just friends now, of course.'

We both laughed at this but I got the feeling that more questions would be unwelcome. Faris's use of the word 'brothers' rather than 'comrades' betrayed his political allegiance, although none of that mattered any more, I hoped. My own connections, by default rather than any informed choice, were on the comrade side, but habit prevented me from revealing anything to Faris. There was a time when internecine fighting between various factions of the PLO was a serious business and many so-called martyrs were created as a result, their posters (produced by printers who must have worked overnight) pasted onto the camp walls for a short while until they were covered over by the latest victims. The Israeli invasion had united everyone in the PLO and the Lebanese Left, creating a grandly named Unified Command. Given my circumstances, though, and my experience with Lazy Eye, I kept quiet.

At the Commodore Hotel I found Bob's Hollywood girlfriend Stacy in the bar, sitting alone and scribbling on a yellow pad, a cold Amstel and a packet of Kent menthols on the small table beside her. There were a couple of men standing at the bar, openly checking her out, wanting her to notice them looking at her. It reminded me of the time my mother had taken me and my brother to a beach south of Beirut, away from the cosmopolitan beach clubs of the city where bathers in bikinis were the norm. A group of men had gathered in the dunes behind us, watching my ultra-blonde and pale mother in her bikini as she lay there, oblivious. I had felt simultaneously embarrassed and protective, wanting to run away and to stay, and ultimately relieved when she became aware of what was happening and got dressed. Remembering the incident made me wince and I glared at the men as I passed them, embarrassed for Stacy. I blushed when she greeted me.

'Doesn't that bother you?' I asked, nodding to the bar. She glanced at the men as if noticing for the first time, then looked back at me. She laughed as she fiddled with her ponytail.

'You're an angel, Ivan, you really are.' She leant forward and lowered her voice. 'To be honest, it's the ones that tell me I'm like a sister to them that bother me.'

I laughed and couldn't think of anything more to say. I asked her if she knew where Bob was.

Bob was stooped over the editing console in the suite at TeleNews, putting together a story on cluster-bomb victims, which he said was a waste of time.

'People in the West don't want to see too much reality over dinner. All the gory stuff gets edited out in London or New York.' He copied a clip of Youssef's wound being changed onto his master tape. 'I think if they showed the real effects of war we wouldn't have it any more. Soldiers would desert when they saw the kind of injuries they were going to suffer. The bomb manufacturers would close down. The whole fucking insalata would stop!' He lit a cigarette, shook his head. 'Well, maybe it wouldn't stop the weapons manufacturers,' he said smiling. 'Those guys would probably pat themselves on the back and buy each other beers if they saw this.' He pointed at a frozen shot of an uncovered, newly created stump where a hand used to be.

I wondered what sort of person became a weapons designer and came up with the idea of a cluster bomb. I must have wondered it aloud.

'The cluster bomb was designed to injure, not kill,' said Bob. 'Some nerdy fucker, probably an Ivy League graduate, came up with the bright idea that if you injure rather than kill someone on the battlefield then they have to be helped, so you reduce the enemy by two or three rather than just one.' He tapped the side of his head to indicate either the intelligence or madness of such logic. 'Of course it's mainly civilians that get fucked.' He ran the video and the shot panned back from the stump to reveal the face of a teenage girl with glazed eyes; it was like something inside had been switched off.

'I think what we need', said Bob, standing up and stretching, 'is the company of a beautiful woman.'

'She's in the bar,' I said without thinking. Bob hooted loudly, thumping me on the back. I smiled, pleased that I'd made him laugh. We got to the hotel to find Stacy deep in conversation with one of the men I'd seen standing at the bar earlier. She was laughing at something he was saying but I couldn't tell whether it was genuine or polite. Bob's smile disappeared and without even slowing down he swivelled on his heels and headed straight back out of the hotel, leaving me standing in the lobby. I was at a loss to understand why and left before Stacy saw me.

9

Youssef and I were watching refugee-camp boys play football on a patch of scrub down the street from the hospital. I'd taken him out for a change of scene after the staff had warned that further filming of 'Girl with Prosthetic Goes to England' would be taking place that afternoon. Youssef's foot was supported by an attachment to his wheelchair; the yellow-stained bandage was dusty and starting to unravel. I wondered whether it was such a good idea to bring him outside. He was enjoying himself though, cheering the boys on and shouting unwanted advice, which for Youssef meant swearing at those who couldn't deliver a decent pass. Profanities flew back at him from the players and he was taunted to get on the pitch and do better himself. You would have thought it was a league match, not six-a-side on dusty ground with a plastic ball that needed inflating.

I sat on an abandoned frame of a chair and smoked, enjoying the weak mid-September sunshine. Youssef went quiet once the game was over and the boys disappeared down one of the narrow alleys of the camp. He wanted to go back to the hospital. I started to wheel him up the road but it was hard in the wheelchair as we had to keep moving onto the rubble-strewn edge to let cars pass. To make sure we didn't get back before the crew had finished I stopped and bought some tea from a man with a cart. As we waited for the vendor to refill our glasses Youssef mumbled something, which I had to ask him to repeat.

'Maybe we should try those crutches again,' he muttered.

'If you think so,' I said, deliberately underplaying my response. Eli had told me that this would happen, that he would come round in his own time and that I shouldn't make a big thing of it. We sipped our tea.

I gave Eli the good news back at the hospital, but she reacted with just a smile and 'OK, good,' before carrying on her treatment of Donkey Man.

'You're not the only one that needs help in this place you know,' I told Youssef, who wanted instant physiotherapy.

'What?! That old man couldn't walk across the room even if there was a naked woman begging him for it at the other end.'

I left him fuming while I found a late lunch in the basement canteen. I avoided Asha and John who were sitting with the hospital administrator, and sat instead with Samir and a nurse I didn't know but recognised from the ward. Samir introduced us and I had to have the usual conversation.

'Is that a Russian name?' asked the nurse. Her name was Fiona; she was Irish. She had a freckled face and copper hair.

'Yes of course.' I excavated my chicken stew, looking for chicken, giving her time to take in my blue eyes and dark hair, my Semitic nose. I saw her compare my skin with Samir's, who I suppose acted as a Middle Eastern benchmark. I was paler than him, but not as pale as her. No one was as pale as her.

'Are you Russian?'

I shook my head. 'And I don't have any Russian ancestors,' I said, hoping to cut out the next question.

'Your English is very good.'

'So is yours.'

She started to apologise, told me that she didn't mean anything by it, she was just curious about where I was from. I let her flounder for a bit while I ate my stew.

'My mother is Danish, my father Palestinian,' I said. 'I went to a school in Copenhagen where they teach English better than the English do, or so I'm told.'

'Do you consider yourself Danish or Arab?' she asked, mopping up the gravy from her stew with flat bread while asking the one question that really vexed me.

Samir interrupted before I could answer. 'He's not an Arab!' he said. 'There's no pride in being an Arab any more. I am Lebanese, I am no longer calling myself an Arab.'

I stood up. 'I am a citizen of the world,' I said. I thought this sounded better than 'I don't know' or 'It depends on who I'm with' or 'Who gives a shit anyway?' Surely a better question would have been, 'What sort of human being are you?'

Later I was standing with Youssef and Eli in the corridor outside his ward. The crutches were not much wider than his legs, which looked like they belonged to an oversized chicken. I lifted him out of his chair and held him up while Eli placed the crutches under his arms. They needed to be shortened, so I held him up some more until Eli was satisfied that they were the right length. You often saw people around the camp walking with splayed crutches because they were too long or, worse still, the crutches were too short and the unfortunate users were bending at the knee to get any support. Youssef, contrary to Eli's instructions of one step at time, launched off as if triggered by a starter gun. I got in his wheelchair and followed him down the corridor as best I could, shouting, 'Go! Go!' in Arabic. Eli was telling me to tell Youssef to slow down but I was wheeling along beside him, caught up in his effort. He was whooping as he went. Reaching the end of the corridor he spun round on one crutch and, because it was easier than standing still, careened forward. With no room to turn the wheelchair quickly enough I was forced to go into sudden reverse, giving my palms wheel burn in the process and almost tipping over as I headed backwards down the corridor. I overtook Youssef and saw him stop and look over my head, wobbling to keep upright.

'You can't catch me,' I yelled, trying to decipher the smile on his face. My wheelchair hit something solid behind me. I looked round to see the hospital administrator rubbing her hip, staring down at me. Any hope that she might have mistaken me for a patient was dispelled when she spoke.

'What are you doing in that wheelchair?' she said, grabbing the handles to prevent me moving forward and escaping. We looked at each other for a moment until I realised that she was waiting for me to get out of the chair. Youssef sniggered as Eli (the professional all of a sudden) led him onto the ward. I was left alone with the administrator. She was one of those people who had no trace of the child left in them. I found such people intimidating and difficult to relate to. 'Who are you?' She squinted at me as if searching her memory.

'I'm nobody, just –'

'There you are, Ivan. I've been looking for you everywhere. Have you forgotten our appointment?' Asha's voice and her arm at my elbow were both welcome, even if it did mean a visit to Intensive Care.

Intensive Care only had three unwilling guests, one of whom was Sharif, the burns victim. My relief at being saved by Asha was cut short on seeing him; his life-support systems were being switched off today. There was a lot of noise coming from his bay, where even more people had gathered round his bed, some of them crying and wailing. The doctor who ran the ICU, a short and wiry-haired Egyptian, was detaching the intubation tube from the hole in Sharif's throat.

The respirator had already been turned off; the heart-monitoring machine was emitting a monotonous note.

'What's going on, Doctor?' Asha asked the Egyptian. 'I wanted to be here when this happened.'

'No need for you to be here. I can do this. I have done this before many times. It is normal.' He was pulling electrodes from Sharif's chest, trying to get the wires round Sharif's mother whose head was welded to her son's shoulder.

'I wanted to be here for the family. I know you can turn the machines off. It was the family I was worried about,' Asha said, trying to comfort Sharif's mother. A couple of women, probably Sharif's sisters, were trying to lift her from the bed. The heart monitor was flatlining in the background. The young woman, who was Sharif's fiancée, according to Asha, and who I had last seen wiping his crusted face, was standing to one side, trying to take everything in, her eyes fixed on nothing. One of the sisters covered Sharif's face with the sheet but this only caused more wailing from his mother. I looked for the off switch on the monitoring machine; the noise was drilling into my ears.

'He is not your patient, this is my ward,' said the ICU doctor.

'You're right, he is not my patient, but I know the family – I told them I would be here for this.'

'You didn't tell me you wanted to be here,' he said.

'Is there a problem?' the fiancée was asking me, gesturing at the two people in white coats standing over her dead fiancé. She was holding a gold chain with a little Koran at the end; maybe it came from Sharif's neck. Her eyes were puffy and her skin pasty. I told her that nothing was wrong, that they were talking of medical things. This must have sounded stupid given that Sharif was dead but she was in another place, she didn't notice.

'The Imam is coming to wash his body,' she said, 'to shroud him before burial. We need to remove his bandages – is that OK?'

I moved to the end of the bed, which Asha and the ICU doctor were now leaning over, both talking at the same time. Sharif's dressings smelt; no one had thought it worthwhile to change them. 'Listen ...' I said, trying to be heard over their overlapping voices, the maternal wailing and the drone of the machine, but I'd become invisible. I tried again in a louder voice: 'I need to ask a question.' This time I got their attention and they looked at me, moving away from one another. In English I told them that the family wanted to prepare the body for burial. The fucking machine droned on. I could now see where it was plugged into the wall.

'Who are you?' the Egyptian doctor asked me in Arabic, deliberately ignoring what I'd just said. Everyone wanted to know who I was, I had to explain myself to everyone. What I wanted to say was, 'Who I am doesn't matter, what matters are the feelings of these people here.' Instead, I just told him I was the translator.

'I don't need a translator,' he said. He smiled at me and looked around for someone to share his stupid joke with. I thought about answering but I did the clever thing and avoided getting into a discussion, understanding that being rational was not top of his agenda. This was understandable, given the previous few months of intensive hell in this place that he called his ward. Instead I moved to the wall and yanked the plug from it, killing the machine, killing the noise.

Back at home electricity came out of the sockets, water from the taps. I was making risotto with an old chicken stock cube I'd found, planning to finish it off with half a packet of butter I'd picked up on the way home. John was in the shower; Samir, Faris and Liv were in the living room. Eli was watching me cook.

'I like being here, in your apartment,' she said as I stirred the risotto.

'Really? Because I'm not sure whether I like attractive Scandinavians being here,' I said.

Her face went blank for a few seconds before realisation flooded it. 'Ah! You are joking with me?'

'Yes, I am joking with you. Help me serve the risotto.'

After eating, Faris read from a two-day-old copy of *The Times* that John had brought with him.

'"According to a United Nations report, between 6 June and 15 August 6,775 people have been killed and 30,000 others wounded. Over 80 per cent of these victims were civilians from west Beirut. According to the same source, 2,094 seriously injured persons had been burnt by phosphor bombs."'

I thought of Sharif, who had started in the last statistic but could, since that afternoon, also be added to the first. A headline on the front read: 'LEBANESE LOATH TO SEE MARINES DEPART'. Samir lit a joint but was the only one who smoked it with any conviction.

'Maybe the war will change the way the world thinks about the Israeli problem,' Faris said, putting the newspaper down.

'Don't you mean the Palestinian problem?' asked Eli.

I caught John rolling his eyes but she was right, that was how everyone referred to it.

'The Israelis are the ones that came all this way to Beirut to try and get rid of us – they are the ones with a problem,' Faris told her.

Eli shrugged.

'The world will be interested for five minutes maybe, then it will all be forgotten,' said John. His face was still pink and blotchy from the shower. 'Even if they manage not to wipe you out.'

'You should wipe that out,' Liv said, poking at John's paunch through his T-shirt. He swiped her hand away.

'They could never destroy us completely,' said Faris. 'Look what happened – all the fighters left Beirut with their weapons and the Israelis had to watch from gunboats. They, more than anyone else, should know you cannot make a people disappear.'

'Then all this war and suffering must continue,' said Eli, as if it had just occurred to her as a possibility.

'The Palestinians are used to suffering – it's in our blood,' said Faris with a grin.

'You don't have a monopoly on suffering,' said Liv, tickling him under the chin. 'People all over the world are the victims of injustice, some get even less support than you do, believe it or not.'

Faris raised his eyebrows at her. He picked the newspaper up and folded it, put it down again. 'You are right, but it is the only suffering we know, we don't know anybody else's.'

An hour later Asha and John decided to go back with Samir.

'Beatles or Rolling Stones?' John asked me as he got up.

I shook my head. I couldn't be bothered with his silly questions; why did you have to choose between one and the other? 'Too difficult,' I said.

'No it's not,' he said, disappointed.

Asha and Samir had already left and Faris and Liv had disappeared into the bedroom. Eli followed John to the front door. I started to clear the coffee table, watched them have a whispered conversation which ended with John shaking his head. Eli looked pissed off. When John had gone I asked her what they'd talked about.

'I just wanted some medical advice, but he is so ...' She waved her hands for the right word.

'Why don't you ask Asha?'

'She's a Catholic.' She took dishes into the kitchen while I tried to work it out. I didn't want to pry. I finished the dregs of wine from various glasses, relit the end of Samir's joint. After a while the power went and we lit candles in the sitting room.

'Do you think it is possible to love two people at the same time?' she asked me.

It was getting late. I stared at the fresh candle burning in the Chianti bottle. I was too tired and drunk to think about it. 'Ah, I suppose so, up to a point. But you could never love them both at the same time. I mean at some point you'd need to choose between them, like if you wanted to go on holiday with one of them or something.' I shut up before it became obvious that I didn't know what I was talking about; obviously hashish and alcohol couldn't give you insights you didn't already have.

'I suppose you are right.' She smiled but in a sad way and I wondered whether I'd said the wrong thing and blown my chances.

'Shall I stay again?' she asked.

'Yes of course, it's too late for you to walk back to the hotel – but I think I'll sleep out here,' I said. Taking her hand I studied her short, neatly cropped nails. I wanted to explain that it wasn't that I didn't want to be with her, but I wanted to be with her in a different way. That I couldn't lie next to her warm, soft and curvy body with her nice-smelling hair in my face without wanting to know what it was like to be with her properly. To be with any woman properly would be good, but with her I thought would be special. It was difficult not to wrestle her to the sofa there and then. Perhaps that was where I was going wrong, maybe I was too timid.

'You are right,' she said, 'it isn't fair to expose you to the temptation of a sexy woman like me without experiencing the full delights.'

I looked at her straight face, eventually remembering to close my mouth. 'You are joking with me?' I said.

'Yes, I am joking with you.' She laughed, took my hands in hers and looked me in the eye. 'I need to sort something out before we can be together, you know, as, ah, lovers.' She blushed as she said this. 'Hopefully tomorrow night,' she added. She got up and tugged at my arms, trying to pull me up from the sofa. 'Let's sleep together again tonight, just one more night. I don't want to be alone. Do you want to be alone?'

No, I didn't want to be alone.

10

At Beirut port, Bob, Stacy and I were just three in a company of maybe a hundred journalists covering the withdrawal of the US marines. I'd not seen that many together since Arafat left from the same spot two weeks ago, passing the same marines that were now leaving. Stacy was waiting with us, a battered reporter's notebook in her hand. They weren't talking, her and Bob, although both of them talked to me. It was an uncomfortable situation, like being with my parents at the dinner table during one of their arguments, arguments that – while his name was never spoken – were always about Karam.

We were all waiting for something to happen. I was standing with a videotape pack round my shoulder, holding a boom microphone plugged into it. I had my headphones round my neck and I was umbilically connected to Bob's camera which perched on his shoulder like a mechanical eye. I fiddled unnecessarily with the sound levels, thinking about what might happen that night if everything worked out with Eli. Bob asked me why I was grinning, but it was Stacy's inquisitive look and her little smile that made me blush. Stacy looked different to me that day, like I was already seeing her in a new light, a light that Eli had tantalisingly shone my way. When she walked over to interview a bespectacled captain, latching onto him with her killer smile, I saw the other journalists (male and female) follow her lazily with their eyes, as if distracted by the passing of an escaped party balloon. By the next morning I hoped to understand what it was they were seeing, rather than relying on my own vivid imaginings. I checked Bob out but he didn't (or chose not to) notice the attention Stacy was getting, preoccupied with some technical colour balancing of his camera against a white wall.

There was a sudden scramble for a small piece of high ground to get the best shot of the last marine getting on the last amphibious transporter. I ended up entangled with a baseball-capped photographer who kicked me in the shins to beat me to a better sight-line.

'Fuck this,' said Bob, putting the camera down. 'There must be a more interesting story to be had in this place.'

I said goodbye to Stacy, who was staying to do more interviews, and we headed back to the Commodore. I asked Bob's regular driver Mahmoud to drop me off near Najwa's road but we got stuck in a traffic jam near the old prison, emptied during the siege. I told Bob that, in the chaos of the Civil War, a rumour went round that all the prisoners were going to be freed on a particular date. On the allotted day relatives started to arrive at the gates to pick up their imprisoned loved ones and, sure enough, the prisoners started to trickle out. The thing was, I told Bob, that the living victims as well as the relatives of the dead victims of those incarcerated had also heard the rumour about prisoners being freed and had also turned up outside the prison. Rather than coming with flowers, they came with guns. Gunfights broke out at the prison gates between those greeting prisoners and those there to settle scores. Some of the prisoners never made it beyond the pavement outside the prison, either being shot down or bundled into a car. It turned out that some of the prisoners refused to leave, deciding that it was safer to stay inside. Bob started chuckling, so I translated it for Mahmoud the driver so he knew what Bob was laughing at. He nodded in recognition.

'Yes yes! That is Lebanon,' he said. They were both still chortling when they dropped me off.

I was surprised to see Najwa's superior, Abu Hisham, open the door to her flat. The last time I'd seen him was in Fakhani, just before the PLO withdrawal, burning documents in sawn-off oil drums. There had been a rushed, round-the-clock attempt to microfilm as many of them as possible before they were destroyed. I assumed the microfilms left during the evacuation. Abu Hisham was the one who convinced me that staying behind in Beirut would be good for me, that I would be useful. At the time it had seemed like a good idea, an opportunity to prove that I could do something worthwhile and be self-reliant for the first time. My mother hadn't been so keen on my staying but the truth was I saw it as a way of escaping my parents and the haunting of Karam's ghost. I could hear Najwa clattering plates behind the closed kitchen door.

'I didn't know you'd stayed behind,' I said, after we'd exchanged greetings.

'I'm just visiting. Wanted to see you before I went back.'

I could see that he was keen on a heart-to-heart in the way he sat opposite me, leaning forward, smiling but appraising. His kindly disposition didn't fool me. I looked out onto the veranda and lit one of Najwa's Kents, offering him the packet.

'Does your mother know you smoke?' he asked disapprovingly.

I smiled and shook my head. He pulled a stick from the packet.

'Have you seen my parents?'

'No. We've been dispersed to the four corners of the Mediterranean. We're still trying to get the infrastructure working again. These are difficult times,' he continued, adopting a more formal tone, dragging on his cigarette and examining it for something to explain its appeal. 'We're all under a lot of pressure, living in these politically and militarily uncertain times, and we are all having to make sacrifices. Now that the multinationals have gone, who knows what's going to happen.'

My mind coasted as he went on about political responsibilities. I was thinking about seeing Eli again that night. I hadn't arranged anything with her in the morning; I'd been asleep when she'd left for her shift, but she'd left a note with the question 'Tonight?' written over a small heart. I felt the need to buy her flowers or something, to make the event special. I wondered where I could get Belgian chocolates in a city that had just come out of a siege. A change in Abu Hisham's tone of voice brought me back to Najwa's sitting room. He was looking at me expectantly, like someone waiting for the answer to a question. I started to feel hot.

'Well, I'm not sure ...' I said, trying to gauge his reaction.

'Have you been listening to anything I've said?' he asked.

'Of course I have.' I knew I sounded defensive.

He raised his hands in exasperation and laughed. 'This is precisely your problem, Ivan, you are always daydreaming.'

I shook my head. 'No ...'

'It's normal at your age to be focused on women and alcohol. But you need to look at the bigger picture, how you can contribute to the wider struggle.' I looked out over east Beirut. 'Don't look so down-hearted, Ivan. You did a good job in Fakhani. Everyone remembers your steadfastness over Black Thursday, don't lose what you have gained because of superficial things.'

I thought back to Black Thursday, manning the radios alone in the Signals basement in Fakhani, the rolling barrage so intense that at its peak I could count an explosion every second. It had started out as a routine night shift with a routine air raid that began towards dawn, but it didn't stop. Six hours of uninterrupted shelling later and the senior cadre on duty in Fakhani had rung through to say he was leaving his post to go somewhere safer and gave me a number to ring in case of an emergency. I wasn't sure what would qualify as an emergency, given the attempted re-creation of the Allied bombing of Dresden, but he'd hung up before I could recover the power of speech. I'd stayed another six hours, alone with the silent Racals and Motorolas. The fighters, who usually radioed in every hour on the hour, had to maintain radio silence in case they gave away their positions to the screaming F-16s above. At one point, with my head between my knees and plaster dust raining down on me, I was convinced that I was going to be buried alive, had even thought about praying to God, until it struck me that if he existed he would be the same God that was making this happen. I looked up to see cockroaches being shaken from the cracks in the wall by the shuddering of the foundations. They scuttled about in confusion, with nowhere to run to.

The bombing had stopped with a sudden and ear-ringing silence. By the time I'd checked with all the hand-helds that everyone was alive I was relieved by the next shift, eighteen hours late due to the viciousness of the bombing. I'd been driven home, had wept with exhaustion and slept for ten hours. The next day the BBC World Service informed me that I'd lived through one of the most ferocious bombing raids since World War Two, stopped only by a telephone call from Reagan to Begin. Now, according to Abu Hisham, I had been mentioned in dispatches for this involuntary episode.

Najwa brought salad, cheese and bread into the room. The grey streak in her hair had disappeared and it was curlier than before, more styled. It was sensible to make herself less conspicuous, I thought. Abu Hisham jumped up to take the food from her. I saw

Najwa give him a smile I'd not seen her use before, coupled with something in the eyes.

'Tonight we will be moving a cadre to your home,' she said, handing out plates.

'Tonight?' I asked incredulously.

Abu Hisham nodded, his mouth full of salad. I tried to hide my dismay by stuffing bread into my mouth.

'We discussed this, Ivan,' Najwa said, exchanging a see-what-I-have-to-deal-with look with Abu Hisham.

'Of course we did,' I said, my voice whiny, 'but I didn't know it was tonight.'

'What's so special about tonight?' Najwa asked.

There was no longer anything special about that night as I sat in my living room, having made up the spare room for my clandestine lodger, replacing the sheets used by Liv and Faris. It was several hours since I'd left Najwa's and I'd since done a stint in John's clinic at the hospital. Eli had come looking for me (usually it was the other way round) and, much to John's disgust, I'd left mid-consultation to speak to her. She'd asked me what time she should come round but I had to come up with an excuse as to why I couldn't see her. Looking back, it must have sounded lame, something about having to visit the family home we'd left during the siege to make sure everything was OK. It was the type of lie that was truth-tinged enough to seem acceptable to the liar; I had promised my parents that I would check on the place. Why I'd prefer to do that than have sex for the first time would have been difficult to explain had she asked. The disappointment followed by bafflement on her face was such that I was tempted to come clean, perhaps by touching on the heroic nature of my deeds; the last scene in *Casablanca* had come to mind. Najwa's face had loomed, however, and I just apologised some more.

'She trying to get you into her knickers then?' John had asked when I'd escaped back into the consulting room. My surprise at his sneering tone must have shown on my face. He told me that she'd asked for help with contraception.

'I told her I wouldn't do it,' he said, 'that it was against my religion.'

I snorted sceptically at this and he added, 'I didn't want to encourage her – besides, why can't she go to a pharmacy like everyone else?' He washed his hands before the next patient, talking to me over his shoulder. 'You know you'd be better off with someone more your own age. There's no shortage of nurses willing to put out for a good-looking guy like you.'

Before I could react he'd called in the next patient and we were dealing with projectile vomit.

My sex life, or lack of it, was public property. Not just that, but people were forming judgements about who I should be seeing. I bet Samir and Faris didn't have this problem. I lit the candle in my Chianti bottle and looked into the flame for insight. Half a candle later and the pre-arranged knock came at the door.

11

I woke just before five in the morning to the sound of screaming jets. But it was just a dream, all was quiet except for the snoring of my secret lodger. I was covered in sweat, and my mood wasn't helped by the fact that I'd had trouble getting to sleep the previous night. Several years ago there'd been a spate of killings, assassinations the Israelis called them, of senior Palestinian officials in Beirut. Often the families had been dispatched along with the targets and for months I'd spent every night tensing whenever I heard the lift coming to life in our apartment block. We kept an AK-47 in a cupboard in the hall (my father didn't qualify for his own bodyguards) and, lying in bed, I would run through a scenario in my head where, at the first sound of crack troops breaking down the door, I would rush for the weapon to defend the family from attack. I'd manage to fight them off and be proclaimed a hero. But then I read that Che Guevara decried heroism as a concept, and so I'd adapted my fantasy so that my actions were acknowledged more subtly, with admiring glances and knowing slaps on the back. At the time I had just returned from two weeks of basic military training, but I knew deep down that my perceived ability exceeded the actual skill and experience needed to rebuff such a professional attack. The fact that my father probably wasn't senior enough to warrant the attention of these secret assassins didn't lessen my fear, and I'd spent many restless nights too much on edge to sleep. Having the cadre in the place had reawakened these fears, except I had no AK-47 here, only an old Tokarev.

My lodger was sleeping off the whisky I'd had to go and buy him after his arrival. I was to be his only contact with the outside world. The whisky was just one item on a list comprising 200 Marlboro, a bottle of Johnny Walker Black Label, a bottle of Courvoisier brandy, aspirin, tinned ravioli, Turkish delight, digestive biscuits and shaving cream. I also delivered a handwritten letter to Najwa, making sure I wasn't followed, which meant taking a half-hour route instead of the ten minutes it would normally have taken. I'd confused the notes (written consecutively on the same pad) and given Najwa the shopping list rather than the communiqué. But luckily she'd read it before I left and I handed over the right one. It didn't do much for my reputation as a revolutionary.

I washed the sweat off with a cold shower – though I couldn't shake the bad feeling from my dream – and dressed, deciding to leave the house early before I was given any more errands to do. I left a note saying I'd be back at lunchtime.

It took me an hour and a half to reach the hospital on foot. Donkey Man and Youssef were the only ones up, patrolling recently disinfected wards. I wasn't sure whether I preferred this smell to the usual sickly stench. Donkey Man had graduated to a walking stick and had managed to shave and get hold of a fresh jallabiyah. He was beginning to look human again. He and Youssef were helping to distribute breakfast to still waking patients, as well as an old man with a stick and a boy on crutches could. The orderly distributing the hard-boiled eggs, bread and tea was more hindered than helped and the whole process was taking twice as long. I exchanged good-hearted insults with Youssef and pulled myself up the stairs to the top floor, where the hospital accommodation, such as it was, was situated. During the siege no one wanted to be on the top floor for obvious reasons and the corridors were strewn with old mattresses (stained with bodily fluids) and out-of-date pharmaceuticals donated by well-meaning but stupid organisations that believed people in crisis would be pleased with whatever they got.

One of the wards had been turned into a dormitory. The administration originally thought that volunteers would be happy to live there but didn't reckon on the European need for privacy and access to restaurants and bars, so the dorm was only used by the needy, desperate or those on call during the night. I knew that Samir sometimes crashed there, sharing the bed of a nurse privileged with the key to the dorm. He omitted to tell them the consequences of being caught with a local in their bed at work. The scandal alone would make coming to the hospital difficult but for some their transient nature in Beirut meant little allowance was made for local sensitivities. In fact many foreigners left common sense at home. I knocked on the door of the dorm and heard shuffling feet before it was opened a crack by Fiona, the Irish nurse I'd met with Samir in the basement canteen. She saw it was me and opened the door a bit wider, looking out to see if I was alone. Her hair was dishevelled and she had a sheet wrapped round her shoulders.

'Samir's not in there, is he?'

She looked blank and I started to regret the question, thinking she might be insulted. She could be one of those celibate Christians – I recalled her saying that she was here with a religious charity. I backed away feeling mortified. She just closed the door and when it reopened Samir was standing there, buckling his trousers and looking down the corridor. I didn't know if he got paid to drive everyone around (I suspect he would have done it for nothing) but if he was found there he would have been fired. We headed downstairs.

Over breakfast I asked him if he would take me to my parents'

place. 'I want to pick up some stuff. I need some warmer clothes.'
My father was probably on a list of people the Israelis had passed on
to their Lebanese agents to make sure they hadn't forgotten about
the evacuation or, if they had, hadn't been stupid enough to stay in
their own homes. I didn't tell Samir all this but since he'd driven
my father around he knew the score. I was keen to leave before Eli
got in to work. I thought I'd feel better if, when I next saw her,
I'd made true the lie I told her the day before. After breakfast we
headed out of the hospital, past the refugees camped in the lobby,
and bumped into Asha alighting from a UNICEF minibus with the
hospital interpreter and what looked like some UNICEF officials.
She stopped when she saw us.

'I hope you two are coming to my new place this evening?' She
showed her impossible teeth. 'I'm cooking Keralan food.'

We both agreed. The interpreter was asking me how I was, smiling
at me in a slightly maniacal way. I was embarrassed because she
was ignoring Samir. Asha wrote the address on a scrap of paper
and slipped back into a more serious manner with her escort. The
interpreter left a trail of perfume. We watched the group as they
entered the hospital. The interpreter was the last to go in. Her jeans
were quite tight.

'Do you think those are Levis?' Samir asked, giving me a deadpan
look. I just shook my head. The guy was impossible. 'She likes you,'
he said. 'She's a Christian, she might let you sleep with her.'

We were travelling in Samir's yellow Mercedes; the taxi sign was
still on the roof. It had the usual charms and trinkets hanging from
the rear-view mirror, including some blue beads to ward off the
evil eye. Samir drove with his left arm resting on the sill, his fingers
only just holding the large steering wheel. His right hand was free
to gesticulate, fiddle with the cassette player and change gear. He
put on some Lebanese pop music and cranked the volume up while

I lit a Benson & Hedges for him. He made a long line of ash on it with a single draw.

'So how is your love life, my friend?' he asked, glancing at me.

'Not as good as yours, obviously.' I watched the ash fall into his lap. 'What's your secret?' I asked, only half joking.

'Not caring,' he said.

I was still trying to figure out whether he meant that he didn't care about the women or whether he didn't care whether he slept with them or not when we pulled into my street. Samir parked the car two buildings down from mine and we sat for a couple of minutes watching the entrance and for anybody lurking on the busy street, which was a collection of featureless modern blocks with shops at street level. I looked up at the balcony of the eighth floor of my building but saw nothing.

'Come on,' Samir said, 'they've either been and gone or have yet to come. What they won't be doing is waiting.' The concierge, Abu Sharif, was sitting in his usual chair inside the entrance of the ten-storey block. He didn't get up when he saw me.

'I thought you'd left,' he said, shifting his bulk and making the chair creak. I held my tongue and Samir pressed the button to summon the lift. 'I thought your father had left the country, no?' He looked at Samir. I nodded in answer. 'But you stayed here?' Abu Sharif had never been quick. I nodded again. 'Going to your apartment?' I tried to think of some withering put-down to this obtuse question but Samir took a break from stabbing the call button and came over.

'Why, is there a problem, old man?' he asked.

'No, God forbid, why should there be a problem? I don't see everyone coming and going of course.' He pointed at me. 'His family have been gone for weeks now and these are strange times. Strangers are in town, come from all over looking for somewhere to live.' He got up and disappeared into his small office, closing the door behind him.

'Something's not right,' said Samir. The heavy concertina door on the lift made a satisfying clanking and clunking, the same noise I used to hear in my bed waiting for assassins. I'd forgotten how slow the lift was; I used to race Karam to our apartment, him in the lift, me on the stairs. I could just beat him if I made him start with the doors closed, because he struggled to open them.

Samir listened at the door as I dug out the key. He gestured to me to listen. I put my ear to it and he smiled as I heard the sound of children inside. I stuck the key in the lock and opened the door.

The first thing to hit me was the mess. We weren't the tidiest of families but the Kurdish cleaner who came once a week made sure the floors and worktops were clean. Now, the living-room floor was covered with plastic bags and open suitcases. The simple Danish furniture, in contrast to the kitsch favoured by many Lebanese, was covered with old clothes. I didn't have time to take in much more as two women in headscarves started shouting and screaming at us from the sofa. Samir was telling them to shut up. We were surrounded by a gang of barefoot children, all yelling foul things at us. Samir tried to swat one of them round the head but its mother shrieked at him, pulling the smirking brat behind her ample behind.

'Get what you need and let's get out of here,' Samir said, fending off children's blows. 'It looks like your concierge has been putting up refugees, probably charging them rent.'

I left Samir shouting, 'It's his house, Auntie. It's his house,' while I rummaged through the wardrobe in my bedroom, pulling some long-sleeved shirts and a couple of jumpers into a duffle-bag. They seemed to have left everything where it was and just covered it with their own things. My parents' room was a pigsty. They'd trashed my father's desk: newspaper cuttings, handwritten foolscap and photos were strewn on top of the desk, the drawers pulled out and emptied, yielding nothing for these people. The yelling had stopped in the other room. I poked around the debris, picked up an old family photo, taken four or five years before my brother Karam's death. We were sitting at a seafront café. It must have been taken by one of those roving photographers who harass people in public places. We were all smiling into the camera, we all looked so young. I turned it over to see 'September 1973' written on the back. I stuck it in my inside pocket with some other photos, righted a bust of Lenin (after whom I was named) and headed for the living room. Samir had found a place to sit amongst the clothes and was drinking coffee served by the women in our cups, made with our coffee pot on our cooker.

The bookshelves, lining a whole wall in the dining room, had been cleared of books and were now home to a black-market operation: boxes of candles, tins of chickpeas, shiny silver flashlights, powdered baby milk, tins of ghee, bottles of Napoleon Five Star brandy, cartons of Marlboro, Winston, Kool, Kent and Benson & Hedges and wholesale boxes of Mars Bars. They were offering me packs of cigarettes and a bottle of whisky but I was gathering my mother's opera records up from the floor. I put them under my arm and told Samir that we were leaving. He picked up his 200 B&U and bottle of Johnny Walker, then put them down again when he saw my face. As we left, I turned and handed the house key to one of the snotty kids standing in the hall. I ran down eight flights of stairs, leaving Samir to wait for the lift. I could find Abu Sharif nowhere.

Back at my apartment, rather than my home, which I'd left for the last time, my lodger was hungry. I went back out again to fetch burgers and fries from a takeaway down the road.

'Good man,' he said, and we ate them in the living room, washed down with warm Amstel beer. 'By the way, someone was at the door earlier,' he said, his moustache shiny with grease. 'A foreign woman, from what I could see through the security hole,' he added. 'That's the type of company you need if you're holed up like this – I nearly asked her in.'

If Samir had said the same thing it would have been funny, but from this older man who looked like an accountant it sounded unsavoury.

'I hope you don't mind,' I said. 'I've arranged to meet her tonight.'

'Like father, like son, eh?'

My lie gave me an excuse not to spend another evening playing cards and drinking whisky. My real plan was to go to Asha's at the AUB. But who knew, maybe Eli had also been invited.

12

The AUB campus occupied a large part of the north-westernmost tip of west Beirut. It would take you at least an hour to walk the perimeter. The high wall that surrounded the campus gave it an exclusive feel, protected from the rest of the city at whose head it was situated. Parts of it were just large tracts of pine trees and bracken. As kids my friends and I could play in whole areas of the campus for hours without coming across anyone apart from the occasional couple of students engaged in heavy petting. Over time we came to know their favourite haunts, staking them out in the futile hope of witnessing some actual sex rather than just hearing about it second-hand.

On a whim I cut into the darkening wood off the well-lit path, following a trail that acted as a short cut between faculty buildings. It reminded me of the ambush lessons in military training and playing hide-and-seek as a kid. One of the thrills was trying to be invisible, part of the undergrowth, wedged into a bush and absolutely still, just waiting. I tried it, squatting behind a shrub off the path, just to see what it felt like again. It felt foolish, hiding when no one was looking for you. I rejoined the path. I couldn't shake the feeling of anger at finding people in our house, even though we were no longer living there. I wondered what my mother would have said – she, veteran of the Christiania squats in Copenhagen, having her own home squatted in. Perhaps she wouldn't have minded, but hopefully she'd be pleased that I'd rescued her records. I hadn't spoken to my parents since they'd left the city or indeed even thought about speaking to them. I wasn't even sure where they were; was it Damascus or Tunis they were going to?

I walked down towards the campus apartments that looked out over the Mediterranean. I'd been here before. They were the same blocks my mother visited every Thursday after Karam's death, while I occupied myself on campus. I never knew which apartment she was in or indeed whom she was visiting, my curiosity dampened by the freedom of a couple of hours to myself. My father later told me she was visiting a 'head doctor'. I would meet her at the edge of the AUB playing field, where older boys pumped iron and did chin-ups, in a hurry to look like men. I wondered, as I sought the right block, who it was my mother had been visiting every week.

Everyone was there, including Eli, who immediately came over to ask me where I'd been. She looked worried and rubbed my arm, letting her hand trail down to the back of mine. I was pleased to see her but wary because I didn't want to lie to her again.

'I came to your place this morning, on the way to Sabra,' she said. Santana was playing in the background. 'Someone was inside; I could see them at the peephole. Was it you?'

John's voice reached me from a bookcase that covered the length of the open-plan living area. 'Ivan,' he shouted, weighing a book in each hand, 'Camus or Balzac?'

'Camus,' I shouted back, having never read Balzac, and glad of a reason not to have to try to explain things to Eli. I got a nod as a reward and Liv handed me a drink with a sway and a smile. Asha was calling Eli into the kitchen but we held eye contact for a few seconds more as I tried to communicate, with my eyes alone, my desperate longing to be with her. Her eyes were full of questions. Asha called again and she was gone. I stepped out onto the large balcony to get air. Standing back from the railing, I admired the excellent view of the sea with the palm-lined Corniche far below, where we had run from the gunfight. Faris sat in a chair smoking, looking out at the gunboats, too deep in thought to notice me. The long fronds of the palm trees swished in the breeze. It was a peaceful contrast to the day's events. Samir released me from my thoughts by slapping me on the back and spilling my drink. Someone turned up the music inside to the guitar riff of a song you just knew was going to explode into something bigger, more exciting. The noise from the large floor-standing speakers made it sound like the group was in the room. We were gripped by a common unspoken urge to dance. Eli was dragging me into the living room while Samir moved the coffee table. Asha grinned and jerked awkwardly, incongruously matched by John's big wavy movements. Even Faris had been pulled into the room by Liv and was dancing with one hand held high, keeping his cigarette out of harm's way. Only Samir refused to dance, but stood at the side clapping his hands in time to the beat. I let myself be consumed by the music and Eli became a blur in front of me as I swung round, my body moving in a way over which I seemed to have no control, as if guitar chords had replaced the signals transmitted by my brain. I felt a surging elation and could hear whooping and shrieking as our whirling became increasingly frantic. The song ended and we all collapsed, laughing and sweating.

Later, when it was too dark to see the sea any more we sat out on the balcony with Ella Fitzgerald's voice easing out through the door. Liv was more animated than usual, her cigarette describing strange figures in the dark.

'The idea of romantic love is nonsense, a myth. If you can't live without someone else that's not love, it's a mental illness,' she was saying.

Eli was shaking her head. 'Then how do you explain the jealousy, the pain of separation or worrying about the other person if they are ill? How do you explain desperately wanting to be with someone?'

Liv nodded her head energetically, eager to jump in. 'Exactly, exactly. You're just describing the symptoms of romantic love. These feelings – jealousy, anger, need – are just about you, not the other person. They are feelings linked with the fear of losing the other person, fear of being alone.'

Asha's voice was measured and calm compared to Liv's. 'Do you remember that man in the field hospital who lost fourteen members of his family all at once?' There were nods round the table. He was a big man whose apartment took a direct hit from a rocket that killed everyone in it apart from him. He'd been impaled on the railing three floors down after being blown out of his house.

'Every day,' she continued, 'he would sit with anyone who had no visitors or was feeling depressed or just come out of surgery. He would talk to them, play cards with them, fetch them water and food.' She hesitated and refilled her glass with water. 'He would hold their hands.' She looked at us and smiled. 'That's love,' she said, 'the rest of it is just ...' She waved her hands dismissively.

'Doesn't your husband mind you being here?' Samir asked her.

'I'm sure he misses me,' she replied, 'but he'd be disappointed if I hadn't come.' She sipped from her glass. 'If he seriously objected we probably wouldn't be together. Can you understand that?' she asked Samir with a smile.

He shook his head.

'He loves you because you are here,' Faris said quietly, continuing to look out to sea.

Asha smiled.

Liv punched Samir playfully on the arm. 'The world is bigger than just two people, you know.'

'My partner hates me being here,' Eli murmured.

I was probably the only one who heard her since she was sitting next to me. I caught her looking down at her hands.

'I only came here for the excitement and the hashish,' said John. Asha raised her eyebrows at him. He leant towards Samir: 'I said I only came here for the excitement and hashish.'

Samir rolled his eyes and reached into his inside pocket. Asha asked how they would get to Sabra from the campus the next day and Samir told her to be at the Etoile first thing.

John sucked on Samir's spliff. 'This place must be the antithesis of Sabra,' he said, waving his hands to indicate the apartment and the campus.

Faris spoke for the second time since dinner. 'Maybe the camps won't be there much longer,' he said.

'What do you mean?' asked Asha. She was piling dirty plates.

'The Phalangists say they want to turn Sabra into ... What do you say? A place for animals,' Faris said. He was looking out into the black, as if addressing some unseen audience. The silent response made him look round and he registered our incomprehension. 'You know, what do you call it, an animal garden? A menagerie?'

'You mean a farm?' asked Liv.

Faris shook his head.

'No,' I tell her. 'He means a zoo. They want to turn it into a zoo.'

I helped Asha with the dishes.

'Ivan, John will be staying in the second bedroom but there's another bed if you want. I don't think he snores.' She smiled and

I thanked her but she hadn't finished. 'I mean it, Ivan, please feel free to stay when you need to. You can stay tonight if you want.' She checked to see that we were alone and took a key from her pocket. It had a keyring with an AUB crest on it, a cedar in a circle. She put it in my hand. 'Only you and John have one of these.' She looked again to the door. 'I know some things may seem exciting at the time, Ivan. But that doesn't mean they're a good idea.'

Samir came in. 'We're going, my friend.'

Samir dropped Faris, Liv, Eli and me off at the Etoile before heading back home, wherever that was. Faris didn't want to go into the bar.

'You don't know who your friends are in a place like this, west Beirut is crawling with lowlife,' he told me in Arabic. Instead we went straight to Eli and Liv's room. The anaesthetist who shared the room was on night shift at the hospital. Faris stripped to his underwear and got into Liv's single bed. Eli and I did the same and hopped into hers. Liv, however, paced the room in her underwear, smoking and talking politics until Eli said something curt in Norwegian. Liv pulled a face but turned out the light and got into bed with Faris. I was feeling pretty exhausted but Faris and Liv were smoking and whispering in bed, giggling. I was spooned behind Eli, watching a pulsing vein in her neck, lit through the window by a weak moon. She smelt familiar, musky and warm. The noises from the other bed, only a couple of metres away, turned into muffled but unmistakable sounds of sex, complete with creaking springs. Eli turned towards me with a disapproving face, sticking her fingers in my ears. I smiled and she leant over to speak into my ear, her hair tickling my face. I looked between her breasts, pale crescents formed by a frayed bra.

'We should go to your place,' she murmured, looking at me, giving me a chance to explain why we couldn't.

'We can't go there. Maybe in a few days, but not yet.' She sank back into the bed and looked at the ceiling.

'I'm going home in two days.' Her whispered words were a blow to the stomach. I felt like crying. Instead, I watched an auburn cockroach cross the wall opposite until it disappeared into a crack. The creaking in the other bed stopped. There was rustling and a sulphur flare lit the room briefly. Cigarette smoke came our way. Eli's breathing slowed and got deeper. I wanted to toss and turn but had no room. I wished I'd succumbed to Asha's insistence that I stay with her and John; I could have been in my own bed now. Overwhelmed with tiredness and wishing I could slip out and go to my own bed I lay looking up at the ceiling, following a crack as far as I could until it was too faint to see.

13

Emile called to me as I turned onto my street. He was with Mustapha and Bedrosian, as well as a couple of other ex-schoolmates. Emile had textbooks under his arm and was wearing an AUB sweatshirt over a buttoned shirt, and I hated him for it. Bedrosian and Mustapha were wearing blazers and trousers, like they were going to a business meeting. A September chill had fallen on the city; I could feel it through my denim jacket and T-shirt. I hadn't slept well; the joys of sharing a small bed were limited without the sex. I fought the urge to run, deciding to sweat instead. I mustn't lead them to where I was staying, not with a cadre hiding there. I didn't have time to think as they crossed the road towards me. I could see mischief in Emile's green eyes.

'Are you on your way to class?' he asked, taking in my dishevelled appearance and lack of books. I'd not prepared an answer for this obvious question. By his smile and the giggles of the others around him, I suspected they knew by then that I wasn't enrolled, but they wanted to hear me say it.

'I'm going to university in Copenhagen,' I said. I was pleased with this inspired thinking and it had the desired effect of wiping the smirks off their faces.

Emile, however, hadn't finished. 'When are you going then? Surely they've started already.'

'No, no, they start much later there. I'm going in a week or so, once everything has been finalised.' I looked up and down the street, hoping for a gunfight or car bomb.

'So which university are you going to?' asked Bedrosian, whose father, I recalled, did a lot of business in Copenhagen.

I searched my memory for the name of a university, frustratingly difficult despite the fact I'd lived there as a child and my mother had lectured there. Bedrosian and Emile exchanged satisfied smiles as they sensed victory.

'Copenhagen University of course, idiot,' I said, banking on the fact that such a place existed. The smiles disappeared and we stood there for a bit, each waiting for the other to leave.

'Where are you off to now?' Emile asked, shifting his interrogation. 'You don't live round here, do you?' Some members of his group were getting bored and started to drift off, telling him they were going to be late for lectures.

'You're going to be late,' I said. I pointed past him to the others and he turned to go, Bedrosian and Mustapha in his wake. To give them time to disappear before I headed towards the apartment I decided to get some breakfast. I started to cross the road to the café on the other side of the road when Bedrosian came running back towards me.

'I almost forgot,' he said, wheezing with the effort of jogging. 'Three of your father's friends came looking for you yesterday.' He caught his breath. 'They were outside the cafeteria, seemed to know that we knew you. Wanted to know if we'd seen you.' He looked at me and sucked air through his moustache, which was growing over his top lip.

'Did they give their names? What did they look like?' I asked, trying to control the panic in my voice.

He looked into the middle distance to show that he was remembering.

'They didn't give names.' He looked round to the receding figures of his mates, turned to go, then stopped. 'So what do you want me to tell them when they come back today? They said they'd come back.'

'Nothing, for God's sake.' I took a deep breath. 'Tell them I've gone to Copenhagen.'

'But you haven't gone yet.' His chubby face was screwed up in puzzlement.

'Tell them I'm going soon. No, don't tell them anything.'

He shook his head, either in disgust or pity. 'I don't know what sort of shit you're mixed up with, Ivan. You were always, I don't know, odd.'

I gave him my best smile.

'Listen man, I hope things turn out all right for you in Copenhagen, if that's where you're really going.' He turned to go. I watched his broad back, saw the others waiting at the bottom of the road. He stopped, put his hand to his forehead and turned round.

'Oh yeah. One of them has a bad eye, looks out at an angle ...'

I was gone before he was finished.

My clandestine lodger didn't seem worried by my story, insisting that I calm down. This was probably why he was a cadre, because of his ability to think under pressure. He asked me to concentrate: did Nabil know where I lived? No, he'd never been here, but could have followed me after the drop. No, if he'd known where I lived they would have been here already, why bother going to the AUB? What would my classmates tell them? Nothing useful. They didn't know I was here. Who did know you were here? Could Nabil have got to any of them and tracked you that way? I didn't think so, he didn't know who my acquaintances were, I didn't think. We worked through the possibilities. The cadre needed to get a message to Najwa. I left him to write something down, went to the kitchen where I saw he'd done all the washing up, cleared out the fridge, even washed the floor. His socks and underwear were hanging on a line he'd rigged across the kitchen. When I went back into the sitting room I saw that that too had been tidied, the coffee table had been cleared. I'd been too wired before to even notice when I'd come in. Something was missing from the table, apart, that was, from all the filled ashtrays and empty bottles. Empty bottles. That's what was missing: my Chianti bottle, carefully sculpted over the summer, had disappeared from the table. He was still writing so I went back into the kitchen. There was a small balcony off the kitchen, big enough for two people to stand on, where he'd put all the bottles. They were all neatly arranged by colour. My bottle was there, but had been stripped of its wax. I took it into the sitting room. My hands were shaking.

'Why did you take the wax off my bottle?' My voice was shaking too. He was putting his letter into an envelope and sealing it. I held the bottle up as evidence of his crime. He laughed, which made me shake even more.

'What the hell is the matter with you, Ivan, are you ill?' he said. 'Do you know what is going on here? Calm yourself, man.' He took the bottle from me and put it on the table. He put the envelope in my clammy hand. 'Take this to Najwa and make sure you're not followed.'

I didn't move. He made a fist and pounded the table. 'Damn you, man, act like your father's son and pull yourself together.' He took off his large-framed glasses, rubbed his eyes for a long while then looked at me. His eyes looked smaller without his glasses. 'Forgive me, Ivan. I'm tired.' The guy's troubles were greater than mine. 'Are you going to be OK?' he asked.

I nodded.

'Good man,' he said.

I took a long route to Najwa's, stopping at Samir's place just to throw off anyone behind me as well as getting something to eat. Samir wasn't there but Faris was, sitting at the table at the back with two of the men I'd seen him in here with before. They looked like they were having a meeting, judging by the serious expressions and haze of cigarette smoke. This time I left him to it; I had my own clandestine affairs to worry about. More and more I felt that I had no control of events unfolding around me, like I was floating helplessly down a river towards a waterfall. Faris joined me at the counter, where I was waiting for a fried vegetable sandwich.

'Have you seen Samir?' he asked. His jawbone was moving rhythmically under his shaved skin. His aftershave was fresh on.

'No, not since last night. Why, what's wrong?'

Faris just shook his head, told me to tell Samir, if I saw him, that he needed to talk to him. I sat at a small table looking out onto the street, watching the people walk by. 'Act like your father's son,' the man had said. Here, everyone was their father's son or daughter, known literally as son or daughter of so-and-so, and remained so until they had offspring of their own when they became father or mother of so-and-so. He'd managed to make me feel ashamed. Whenever I was told not to forget who my father was I knew I was being told that I didn't measure up to him. I ate my sandwich and tried to concentrate on the present.

Najwa was surprised to see me, and didn't look that pleased, although to her credit she covered it up well. Not quickly enough that I didn't see her glance over my shoulder to see if I was alone, that I hadn't led Nabil and his cronies to her. I gave her the letter and went out onto the balcony to sit at the table. I smoked a cigarette and looked out to east Beirut until she called. Abu Hisham was there, still in his pyjamas. He must have been in the bedroom when I'd arrived. We went over the same ground I'd been over with my lodger; I couldn't find anything to tie Nabil back to my apartment.

'Just to be safe we should move him out,' Abu Hisham said. 'His classmates can tie Ivan back to his street, so we should assume that the dog Nabil will do the same.'

'Maybe it's safer to leave him where he is,' said Najwa. 'Since they could be watching the street, they could spot him leaving.'

'No, it'll only be a matter of time before they find the right building. There are enough people with a grudge against us to provide this information for nothing, never mind if they start waving money about.'

They put together a plan for evacuating the lodger. Other things needed to be organised, not least where he was to go next and who was to take him in. I wasn't privy to this part of the conversation but was sent back to explain the plan to the cadre, as he was to leave late that night. I walked past the entrance to my apartment building twice: the first time I was suspicious of someone standing inside the entrance (who turned out to be a resident waiting for an elderly relative to descend the stairs) and the second time I was spooked by someone sitting in a car on the opposite side of the road (who was subsequently joined by his wife and kids for whom he was waiting). Realising that I was probably attracting more attention walking up and down outside the building I darted inside.

Later that afternoon I couldn't find Bob in the TeleNews offices so I headed across the road to the Commodore. The lobby was full of Lebanese drivers waiting to transport their journalists to film the departure of the French paratroopers, the last of the multinational force to leave. He wasn't there either so I went to the bar where I found Stacy, sitting at her table with her yellow pad and menthols. I went and sat down opposite her. She looked genuinely pleased to see me, her smile like an injection of good feeling. The smile quickly disappeared, however, when I asked about Bob.

'Bob could be anywhere,' she said. Her drawl was raspy from too many Kent Menthols. She retied her ponytail. 'He could be anywhere in this hotel, or in any other hotel for that matter,' she said with a short bark of a laugh.

I said nothing. I noticed a packed suitcase by her chair. She took a Kent from the packet and I managed to light it for her without setting fire to anything else. She arched her back and stretched her neck to blow smoke at the ceiling. This made her T-shirt tighten against her chest. When I raised my eyes she was looking at me and smiling.

'How old are you, Ivan?'

'Eighteen.'

'Eighteen. You must have a girlfriend, right?'

I hesitated – did Eli count as a girlfriend?

'I can't believe a good-looking boy like you hasn't got a girlfriend or two?'

I smiled but inwardly winced at the word 'boy'. I knew that she wouldn't say something like that if she thought of me as a serious proposition. Maybe she was right, maybe I was still a boy.

'Don't become like the rest of them, will you?' she said, serious all of a sudden. She crossed her arms on the table and leant forward to look intensely into my eyes. I had to move my gaze to the table in embarrassment.

'Naw, I don't believe you will.' She picked up her pen.

'Bob's a fool,' I said, blushing as hard as I could.

She smiled and leant forward and I thought, hoped, she was going to kiss me. But she didn't, she just tapped my fingers with her pencil.

'Thank you, young man. Now go away, I have to file my final piece on this city in an hour.'

'What's it about?' I asked, looking at her neat handwriting. I wasn't genuinely interested but just wanted to prolong our conversation and make the people in the bar think there was something between us.

'It's about some Jewish women living in Sabra, who married Palestinians before 1948. They came with them in the exodus. I've managed to track six of them down.'

I stood up and pointed at the suitcase. 'So where are you going?'

'I'm flying home for a few days then I'm going to Nicaragua. It's where the next story is.'

I wasn't even sure where Nicaragua was but I wanted to go with her, carry her bag for her, sharpen her pencils, light her cigarettes. She smiled her devastating smile and waved me away. I never saw her again.

14

The cadre's transfer went smoothly. The only awkward bit was when we had to wait inside the lobby to my building. I kept popping out onto the street to have a look for the car, a red Peugeot 405 driven by a man in a beret.

'Relax, he'll come,' said the cadre.

'He's late,' I said.

On my third foray onto the darkening street I spotted the car crawling down the road, the driver looking for the fast-food restaurant that was the agreed meeting place. The restaurant was two buildings down from where we were; hopefully far enough away from my place so that no association could be made by whoever was picking us up, but close enough so that the lodger didn't have far to walk, which was a risk in itself. The Peugeot double-parked outside the restaurant. I went into the lobby.

'He's here. I'll take your bag, you follow when I'm at the car,' I said. I placed the bag on the back seat of the Peugeot and left the door open. The cadre slipped into the car, closed the door and wound down the window.

'One moment, comrade,' he said to the driver, before turning to me. 'Thanks for your hospitality.'

'It was nothing.'

'Good man. You'll fill your father's shoes yet.'

Then he was gone.

Now I was in the Etoile lobby. I could see Samir in the bar but headed upstairs to Eli's room. She was there with Liv and three other women I didn't know. They were sitting round the Irish girl Fiona, who for some reason was wearing sunglasses, cradling a glass. The room reeked of whisky. They looked at me as I entered the room but nobody smiled or greeted me. I had interrupted something. I tried to dispel the awkwardness with a joke about Fiona looking like Jane Fonda, which she did a bit in the glasses. Nobody laughed though and I saw Eli trying to shoo me away with discreet movements of her hand and wide eyes. Fiona, however, raised her head to look at me, taking off her glasses. Her left eye was puffed and filled with blood with a blue and black ring under it like she hadn't slept for years. Eli was mouthing 'Samir' to me as I backed out of the room feeling hated, like I'd done it myself. Now I knew why Faris was looking for Samir. What I didn't understand was why Samir was here at the Etoile.

I went downstairs and saw him standing at the bar with two blond men. At a table with their backs to me were a couple of Arab men in leather jackets, watching Samir. As I approached the bar the blond men were smiling politely at an obscene joke Samir was telling. He laughed too loudly at the punch line, his gestures over the top. One of them spoke to the other in Swedish; they were probably with the Red Cross. I smiled at them, asked in pidgin Swedish if they wouldn't mind if I talked to my friend here for a minute. They looked relieved at being able to go without causing offence.

'What are you doing here? Do you know who's upstairs?' I said in Arabic to Samir.

'Brigitte Bardot?' He chortled into his whisky, avoiding eye contact.

Looking past Samir into the lobby I could see Faris. He was about to come in, then saw the two men sitting at the table. My gaze followed his and I saw they were looking at Samir and me with great interest. One of them nodded at me as if I knew him. Faris shook his head at me and pulled an angry face, pointing at Samir's back. Then he bounded up the stairs, three steps at a time.

'Let's go to my place,' I said to Samir in a low voice. 'This is not a good place to get drunk.' I took his elbow.

'What's your secret, Ivan?' His voice was loud enough to stop the chatter in the bar for a few seconds. Without looking to check, I imagined the two men at the table nudging each other and taking out notebooks, giving each other the thumbs up. 'What's your secret with women?' He must have been drunker than I thought. I led him towards the lobby. 'They tell me I should be more like you,' he said, although thankfully he was mumbling now.

'Come home with me and I'll tell you all I know about women. I have notes and pictures and everything,' I said. I led him out of the bar, thinking he was the one who should be giving me advice about women. I suggested we walk back but he wouldn't hear of it, insisting on going to his car. He was in no state to reason with.

Amazingly, Samir was transformed behind the wheel of his Mercedes. It was as if he could negate the effects of alcohol with the mechanics of driving. Besides, I was sure that he wouldn't have let me drive even if I could; he could never tolerate being a passenger.

Ten minutes later we were inside the apartment and he collapsed on the sofa. I made coffee.

'This is shit,' he said, pulling a face. I had to agree with him. The coffee grounds were like fine sand and plastered the back of my throat. The caffeine still worked, though; I felt my heart knocking in response to its effects.

'Why did you do that to Fiona? What happened?' I asked.

Before he could answer someone thumped at the front door, too loud and prolonged to be friendly. Samir and I looked at each other. I was thinking of the two men in the Etoile bar; I'd been certain they hadn't followed us out of the hotel.

'Do you have a weapon here?' he asked.

I pulled up a chair and got the Tokarev down from its hiding place and handed it to Samir, relieved that he was using it and not me. The only thing I'd used it against were rats – huge dirty things that roamed Fakhani like they owned it. Rat shooting was something Samir and I had done together before. The knocking resumed with more vehemence. The neighbours were going to wake up if it carried on. Samir looked incredulously at the Tokarev as he removed the safety and loaded a bullet into the breech.

'Is this the same piece of shit that jams every third shot?' he asked.

I nodded.

He shook his head, disgusted. 'Then let's hope there are only two of them.' He went to the hallway, steady on his feet, incredibly. I followed, feeling safer behind him than staying in the sitting room. He turned off the hall light and peered through the security peephole, pressing the muzzle of the automatic against the wooden door at chest height. I couldn't see his expression to judge what he could see. To my surprise he whipped open the door wide. The landing outside was dark and I couldn't see past Samir but heard a smack and a grunt and I had to step back to let him fall on his backside in front of me. Faris was revealed in the doorway, rubbing his clenched fist. He came in, silently closing the door behind him. He only had eyes for Samir, who was holding his face with one hand

and the Tokarev with the other. Faris picked Samir up by the shirt and I stepped aside as he dragged him past me into the sitting room. He pulled him up onto the sofa so that he was slouched back where he was before he got up to answer the door. He stooped and stuck his face in front of Samir's.

'You hit a woman again and I'll split you open lengthways,' he said quietly, as if asking him to stop leaving his socks lying around. 'Do you understand what I'm saying, you stupid shit?'

Samir nodded, tears streaming down his face.

Faris noticed the Tokarev in Samir's hand for the first time. 'What are you doing with that?' Samir handed him the gun and Faris removed the magazine which he put on the table, then pulled back the breech to release the loaded bullet, which clattered onto the marble floor. He pointed the Tokarev at the wall and dry fired it, to make sure nothing was in the breech. He put it on the table. 'You could've killed someone with that.'

'There were some suspicious men at the Etoile bar, we were a little edgy,' Samir said.

'You were right to be. It was raided.'

'Who by?' Samir asked.

'I didn't wait to find out. I escaped through the girls' window.' He went into the kitchen, where I heard water running. I picked up the bullet from the floor and pressed it into the magazine, then slipped the cartridge back into the Tokarev. Faris was back with a wet tea towel. He gave it to Samir to dab his eye, which was starting to swell up.

'How about some coffee?' Faris asked, looking at me for the first time, as if I'd just appeared. He rubbed the knuckles on his right hand.

'His coffee is shit,' Samir said. 'How about some whisky?' He blew his nose into the tea towel and handed it to me. 'A new one would be an act of human kindness.'

We played cards, Faris occasionally looking at Samir and shaking his head with a wry smile as if Samir were his hapless and less intelligent younger brother. For the first time I got a sense of how close they were. Several hands of cards, half a bottle of Johnny Walker and an ashtray full of stained filters later, Samir and Faris decided to leave. Samir went to the bathroom to check his eye while Faris put the cards away.

'Why did you do that to Samir, couldn't you have just talked to him?' I asked Faris in a low voice.

He shrugged, making a cigarette jump from his soft pack of Marlboro by flicking his wrist. He lit it and checked the filter, looked me in the eye. 'That's what he should have done with Fiona. You should never hit a woman.' He looked away and blinked frantically as if trying to get something out of his eyes; I'd never seen him so unsure but before I could question him further he asked, 'Why are you still here, Ivan?'

'What do you mean?'

'I mean you don't need to be here, in this city. You have a foreign passport, no?'

'Yes I do, but –'

'Then you should be in Europe, studying. Did you know I went to the Sorbonne in Paris?'

'For real? What did you study?'

'International law,' he said, smiling. 'But seriously, Ivan, you have choices, you should consider them.'

Samir was back in the room. His right eye was now a dark red.

They left shortly after three in the morning and I considered going to bed, but I was too jazzed up. Instead, since the electricity was on, I picked out one of my mother's opera records, one with a woman dressed as a gypsy on the cover. I sat all the way through it, at first as a test of perseverance, but after a while I was absorbed in the music. I could feel myself drifting off to sleep on the sofa as it began to get light outside.

Soon there was buzzing in my ears, like a bad-tempered mosquito. I swatted at the noise but it just got louder and turned into ringing. I woke on the sofa – it was the doorbell. The needle on the turntable was cutting a new groove into the end of the record. Eli was on the other side of the peephole. I opened up and she took in my hair and clothes.

'Still asleep?' she asked, coming in with a plastic bag. 'I have breakfast.' She held up the bag and my hunger hit me, catching up with me from the day before. I made tea while she fried eggs. I asked her why she wasn't at work. She told me she'd taken the morning off.

'I want to say goodbye to people before I go. I'm going to work this afternoon.' We dipped the fresh bread in the salty yolks, sharing a plate. She let me mop the plate up. I gulped the hot tea and leant back into the sofa.

'You were hungry,' she said. We were sitting next to each other. She was wearing a perfume that she'd bought from a market stall in the camp and her braids had black ribbons in them. She sipped her tea. I was agonisingly aware of how close she was, of her jasmine scent.

'How's Fiona?' I asked.

'She'll live.'

'Did she say why it happened?'

'Does it matter? It shouldn't have happened.'

I told her about Faris and Samir; how Samir now had the same black eye as Fiona. She looked unconvinced.

'Samir will probably lose his driving job with the Red Crescent,' I said. I didn't know why I was defending him. I just wanted everyone to get on, like before.

'I'm not sure Fiona will make a complaint. Maybe if she sees him she'll think they're even.' We smiled at the image of them meeting.

I sensed an edginess between us as we made small talk. It was like a physical tension that was waiting for the right trigger to snap and be released. I didn't know what that trigger was or what to do. I was worried that it would go away, an unknown opportunity lost for ever, or that I would dispel it with the wrong word or gesture. But Eli knew what to do. She took my hand, got up and led me to the bedroom. I stood by the bed paralysed as she wound down the shutter, restricting the sunlight to narrow strips on the bedcover. Then she was undressing and helping me undress until we were standing naked before each other. She was looking me up and down and smiling at my erection which felt like it would explode and kill us both. She pulled me onto the bed and things were happening more quickly. She was guiding my hands and my mouth. My senses were overwhelmed by her smooth curves and smells and softness and whispers. I was immersed fully in the experience; nothing else in the universe mattered, nothing at all. Soon I could hear people crying out and something was welling deep in my pelvis. Then I got the flash I had before my fit and an explosion ripped through me, again and again. When I opened my eyes I was still alive and looking down at Eli to make sure she was OK. Her eyes were unfocused and she was breathing rapidly through her parted lips.

'Next time,' she said, her voice coming from somewhere deep in her chest, 'we'll try to take it more slowly.' We lay next to each other for a minute, catching our breath. She started guiding my hand over her breasts and down her damp belly; 'next time' was happening now.

At some point we had lunch and at some point we shared a cold shower which served to rejuvenate us to try it all again. Now we were lying on our backs on the bed after an involuntary nap. Eli looked at her watch, the only thing she was wearing apart from her redundant wedding ring, which she took off and handed to me.

'This may be useful,' she said. 'In case you need to sell it or something. It's good quality.'

'I would never sell it.' I tried it on my fingers but it was either too big or too small so I laid it between her breasts and watched it rise and fall for a bit.

'What are you going to do, Ivan?'

'I'll get a chain for it to wear round my neck,' I told her, but I knew she wasn't asking about that. She raised herself on one elbow to face me. I searched for the fallen ring in the crumpled sheet.

'Seriously, Ivan.'

'I don't know – something will turn up.'

'No, you can't just wait for things to happen to you. Have you thought about going back to Denmark?'

I shrugged and pulled the sheet up over myself.

'Do you have someone you can stay with? Where are your parents?'

I studied the light through the slats in the blind. It had faded to a grey that meant it must have clouded over or else it was getting late.

'I can give you some money to buy a ticket – I have money.'

I knew then that something between us was lost that could not be recovered. She'd taken on a different persona, behaving like a concerned aunt rather than a lover, sounding like Faris with his questions. The doorbell went and I welcomed the opportunity to slip on my jeans and go down the hall. Liv was trying to look the wrong way through the peephole.

'Is Eli here?' she said, her face all serious. I nodded and she headed past me for the bedroom before I could say anything. I followed to find her sitting on the bed next to Eli, who had covered herself with the sheet. The room smelt of sex.

'Have you heard the news?' Liv asked. We looked at her. 'There's been a big explosion in east Beirut, at the Phalangist headquarters. They say that Bashir Gemayel has been killed.'

15

Samir was waiting in the car to take us to Sabra. Depending on which radio station you tuned into, Bashir had either definitely survived or definitely died. But by the time we got to the hospital it was clear that he had been killed, along with twenty-four other Phalangists, in an enormous explosion (even by Beirut standards) which had pulled down the building he was in.

At the hospital we had a little gathering on the orthopaedic ward for Donkey Man, who was being discharged into the camp and the care of his relatives. The nurses gave him a new walking stick and Asha shook his hand, saying he was her longest-staying patient. He had a new kufi on his head and tears in his eyes as he told me to thank everyone. Youssef was there, circling the get-together on his crutches, cursing and muttering.

'He's going mad here,' I told Eli.

'As his physio I recommend sea air. Why don't we take him to the Corniche tomorrow?' she suggested. 'I'll have time before my flight if we go in the morning.'

I told Youssef the good news.

'The sea? What do I want with the sea? I want to see a film,' he said.

I told her he was delighted with the idea.

She laughed. 'I can tell from his expression.'

I left Eli to say some goodbyes and went to work in the clinic.

We met up at Asha's for dinner. Afterwards we went back to my place and I put into practice what I'd learnt earlier that morning. Eli told me I was a good student.

Low-flying and screaming Israeli F-16s woke me from a deep and nourishing sleep – this was no dream. Eli was next to me, naked on her last day in Beirut.

'Are they bombing?' she asked, pulling the sheet over her chest.

'No, they're just breaking the sound barrier. All the terror without the destruction. Well, apart from some broken windows.'

After a wordless breakfast we walked to Samir's falafel place where we'd agreed to meet him before picking up Youssef. Samir wasn't there but among the regulars I saw Faris huddled with his 'brothers' at the back table. He hadn't seen me so I approached, catching him drawing a map on a paper napkin.

'I can't see any other way,' he was saying. 'We can't stand by while ...' He saw me and flipped the napkin, then stood up.

'Ivan. What are you doing here?'

'Waiting for Samir.' As if on cue, squealing announced a Red Crescent ambulance stopping outside. Samir jumped out of the driver's side. He came in, his eye now black and blue.

'A woman finally teach you some respect?' someone asked.

'Exactly so,' he said, without smiling.

Faris and I joined Samir and Eli at a table.

'You won't be going home today,' Samir told Eli. He helped himself to a cigarette from my pack. Eli and I looked to Faris.

'The Israelis are invading the city,' Faris explained. 'The airport is closed.'

There went Youssef's chance to see the sea. The regulars crowded round our table, firing questions: How far away were they? Would they come into the Hamra district? Faris just shrugged. They started to drift away.

'I should go to the Etoile, find out what's happening,' Eli said.

'Good idea,' Faris said. I felt I should check in with Najwa and find out what I should be doing but instead I told Eli I'd walk her to the hotel. Faris called to his friends. We all spilt onto the street. Faris got in the passenger side of the ambulance while his mates got in the patient end. Samir shouted instructions for his café to close. He got in the driver's side and the ambulance accelerated onto the road, the siren wailing into life but dying seconds later. I imagined an exasperated Faris telling Samir to turn the fucking thing off.

At the Etoile a man from the Norwegian embassy was addressing a mixed group of Westerners in English, telling them that there was nothing to worry about as long as they stayed in the hotel. He took the details of those whose departure had been delayed so he could let their charities know. As soon as he was done Liv stood on a chair.

'The last thing I'm going to do is stay in this hotel,' she declared in English. 'I suggest we go to the camp – the more Europeans there the better.' She pulled her black hair into a tight ponytail as if preparing to go for a long run.

'Why, what do you think is going to happen?' asked Fiona. Even with her shades on her anxiety was clear.

'I don't know exactly, but history tells us that it won't be anything good.' She lit a cigarette, puffing impatiently, and a multilingual discussion about what to do broke out. In the end half the people there decided they should go to the camp. Fiona, however, had already left the room. Liv joined Eli and me.

'I'll go with you,' Eli said to her.

'Are you sure?' I asked.

'She's right, Ivan, we can't sit here. Also, Youssef is there, remember.'

I nodded.

Liv hugged Eli and went to convince some others. I squeezed Eli's hand and left for Najwa's.

Najwa filled me in on what she knew: apparently the Israel Defense Forces were advancing along three fronts and would be in the streets below by tomorrow.

'After all, who will resist them now – the fighters have gone, the mines have been cleared and most of the weapons handed over to the Lebanese army.'

She might as well have been talking to herself, pacing up and down in a trail of cigarette smoke. I yawned, feeling the effects of yesterday's marathon. I wondered, now that Eli's flight was cancelled, whether we'd be able to do it all again that night. I felt a pang of shame; we were being invaded and Eli's flight home had been cancelled and all I could think about was sex. Najwa was handing me a package; it was to go to Dr Ramina at the American University Hospital.

'Probably the last for a while,' she said, as I tried to stuff the large envelope into my jacket without success. This time there'd been no attempt to camouflage it in newspaper.

The streets weren't as busy now and most shops were closed or closing, the shutters clattering to the street in a burst of metallic noise. I turned onto my street, thinking I would cut through AUB to the hospital, which lay to the east of the campus. Halfway down the street and someone was shouting my name from a shiny black Mercedes coming towards me. I could see an arm waving from the back window but couldn't see through the front screen due to the late sun reflecting on it.

At first I thought it must be Emile or one of his cronies, but when the car drew level I saw only strangers in the front, clean-shaven men in leather jackets. They were smiling. I stopped, peering into the back, and saw Lazy Eye Nabil alongside another man. He smiled when his good eye met mine and he started to open the door before the car had even stopped. My instinct was to turn and run but a calmer part of my brain told me to run in the direction I was walking, as they would have to reverse – already another car was pulling up behind them making that difficult. As I pulled away I knew I could easily outrun Lazy Eye, but I was panting by the time I reached a side street. I risked a look as I turned into it and saw them getting back into the car, yelling at the driver behind them to get out of the way. They were going to try to follow me in the car.

I ran as the whine of the reversing Mercedes' engine followed me down the road. I heard a screech of brakes, some horn blowing and swearing but I didn't stop to look. I reached the entrance to an alley and glanced back to see the Merc just turning onto the side street. I jumped into the alley, gambling on the fact that they were too far away to see me, and came to what looked like a dead end – a courtyard overlooked by apartment blocks on three sides and a high wall on the fourth lined with overflowing rubbish bins.

It was dead space; no doors into the apartments. I could hear the car coming down the street and climbed onto a putrid-smelling bin, disturbing some rats inside. I scrambled over the wall and landed on a patch of dirt, scattering some emaciated chickens. The chickens beat their scrawny wings in a hopeless attempt to fly. I was in a courtyard. I couldn't hear the car any more but my heart was thumping too loudly and the courtyard echoed with squawking. I gestured desperately for them to settle down, but that only set them off again. I was still clutching the stuffed envelope from Najwa, now damp with sweat. It had torn and I could see Lebanese passports inside. I sat against the wall I'd just jumped over, trying to slow my breathing, thinking of the Tokarev sitting uselessly in the apartment. I could see an iron gate which covered a door into a shuttered house but it was padlocked. My eyes stung from the sweat dripping off my forehead. I heard footsteps on the other side of the wall. I badly needed to urinate.

'Are you sure he came in here?' a voice asked.

'No, the shit could have gone into any of the buildings on the street,' said Lazy Eye in resignation.

'Come on, let's go, he's not worth it,' said the first voice.

'It's who he can lead us to,' said Lazy Eye.

'Can you hear chickens?' said the first voice.

'Come on, you guys,' called a third, more distant voice.

The footsteps receded and it went quiet and the voices started up again but were too far away to make out what was being said. A car started and drove away. The chickens had calmed down; they were pecking fruitlessly in the dust. They looked as though their feathers had been nibbled and plucked, probably by rats. I waited for a long time before crawling on my knees to pick up a rusty tin lid. I used it to start digging in the dirt, making a hole big enough for the envelope, which I buried and covered. Only then did I piss against the wall, easing the pressure in my bladder. The wall looked impossibly high from this side and I had to take a running jump at it, clambering until I could get a leg over the top. It was only when I was on the other side that I stopped to think about where I should go. I looked for cigarettes, finding Asha's key on the AUB keyring in my pocket. Her flat was the safest place I knew.

By the time I found the courage to emerge from the alley the streets were empty and it was starting to get dark. I walked as fast as possible to the AUB, avoiding my street. I had to convince the guard at the gate that I was allowed to enter, pretending that I couldn't speak Arabic to avoid awkward questions. I realised that my mock outrage at being stopped didn't sit well with my appearance, but the passport and AUB keyring seemed to convince him.

Once inside I was glad the apartment was empty. In the bathroom mirror I could see why the guard was reluctant to let me pass. The knees on my jeans were covered in ground-in chicken shit. My hands and wrists were scratched and my face was covered in dirt streaked by dried sweat. I made full use of the facilities then helped myself to the owner's Canadian Club whisky. I even found ice in the freezer. Standing at the balcony door I lit a cigarette and held the whisky-flavoured ice in my mouth as long as I could. The BBC World Service led on the fact that Grace Kelly had been in a car accident. That was followed by an item on the entry of the IDF into west Beirut in order to 'restore order' after the vacuum left by the assassination of President-elect Bashir. No traffic was visible on the Corniche below. I was starting to relax with a second Canadian Club when I heard a distant rumbling that kept stopping and restarting, getting louder all the time. Then, through the palm trees lining the Corniche, I could see an Israeli tank, a sand-coloured Merkava, growling to a halt. It waited, then moved forward about a hundred metres before stopping again, spewing black smoke into the air. Soldiers followed behind, helmeted and wary, and I instinctively dropped to the floor of the balcony, worried that I might be seen. This then was the enemy, I thought; at last, we got to see them after experiencing their firepower for weeks. I had seen them before, but through binoculars across no-man's-land at the airport, the shimmer of the August heat distorted by the lenses, making them look ghostly and unreal.

Now here they were, entering Beirut for the first time, with no resistance, just driving up the fucking Corniche without so much as a shot being fired. I watched as a column of these mechanical beasts tore up the tarmac. Eventually the line stopped and after a while the engines switched off to leave a stunning silence. Then, as if the whole event was being choreographed, the electricity cut out and the whole city went black.

Inside I lit some candles and, not knowing what to expect, burnt the photos of my parents that I'd rescued from our home. I kept just one, the one of all four of us taken in 1973, where we all looked so young.

16

I was woken at midnight by knocking, and staggered to the door, half expecting Asha or John. It was Samir. He came in and collapsed on the sofa, looking like he'd seen the devil.

'They're everywhere,' he said, after catching his breath; I handed him a live cigarette and a beer from the still cold refrigerator. 'They've surrounded the camp, no one's allowed in or out – I've just tried to get back in.'

'Where are the others, where's Faris?' I asked.

'I don't know. I dropped him and his friends in the camp this morning. Asha and John were already at the hospital; Liv and the others arrived later. I brought some of the others back to the Etoile. Then I tried to go back but couldn't get in – the Jews have roadblocks everywhere.'

'Maybe Faris is in hiding,' I said.

'No, he's in the camp somewhere. Waiting.' I watched his Adam's apple bob up and down as he gulped his beer.

'Waiting for what?'

'I don't know, maybe the Israelis are planning to enter the camp at some point – the hospital is full of people from the camp, just come to spend the night, scared shitless.'

I told him about the tanks so we went and sat on the balcony in the dark and watched them far below. Nothing moved, but the dim moonlight made it possible to see their outlines.

'You could take one of those out with an RPG from here,' Samir said, a little too loudly for my liking. He was on his feet, measuring distances and angles with his hands.

'You'd only get one shot before they blew the apartment away,' I told him, worried that he'd talk himself into doing it for real. He sank back into his chair and we sat for a bit until it got too cold.

For the second day running I was woken by low-flying jets, their sonic boom reverberating over the city, a reminder of the terror they could inflict. I watched the window over the bed rattle, grateful for the criss-cross of tape on the glass. I found Samir standing on the balcony in his underwear drinking coffee, watching F-16s fly out to sea over the gunships. The column of tanks had disappeared from the Corniche below. I poured coffee and sat down, feeling uneasy at him standing by the railing.

'I wonder what happened to that Soviet battleship?' I said.

Samir shrugged dismissively. Throughout the siege, the Soviets had positioned a battleship offshore to monitor events. At times we'd wished they'd done more than simply watch. I didn't understand how anyone could have let things carry on as they did, least of all the self-proclaimed peace-loving Soviet regime. An American battleship joined them at some point but neither saw fit to stop the Israeli gunships pummelling the city.

'Like all the other fuckers, they don't care what happens here; not enough to do anything – I mean really do something, not fuck about at the UN.' He lit a cigarette. 'Do you think they would just watch if these things happened to them, in their country?' he asked.

I'd lived long enough in Denmark to know that most people there, or indeed in the rest of the world, probably didn't give more than a passing thought to what went on here, beyond what they had to sit through on the news, and even that was watered down and sanitised, according to Bob. But I wondered how much Samir cared about what went on elsewhere in the world. Maybe Liv had the right idea with her internationalist outlook. Maybe you couldn't fix things in one place without fixing them everywhere.

'I'll tell you what needs to happen,' Samir was saying. He turned away from the sea and came over to me. 'They need to experience what we experience.' He prodded me in the chest. 'Do you know what we should do?' he asked.

'What?'

'Have some breakfast.'

We fried some eggs and Samir made some fresh coffee. After we'd eaten and lit up I told him that I needed to get some things from my place.

He studied me. 'Can't go back, my friend?'

'Do you remember Nabil?' I said.

'The guy with the eye? Yes, I haven't seen him since the siege.'

'He works for the Israelis. He spotted me near the apartment.'

'That son of a whore. That fucking son of a dog whore.' He shook his head. 'I always knew he was bad.'

'You did? How so?'

He pointed at his eye. 'He looked wrong.'

Later we were sitting in Samir's yellow taxi two blocks from my house.

'Give me the keys,' he said, holding out his hand.

'Are you sure you want to go?'

'I drove your father around for over three months, my friend. When he left he told me to keep an eye on you. Give me the keys.'

I gave him the keys and told him what to get.

'I'll be twenty minutes.'

I looked at my watch, switched on the radio and moved the dial. I didn't know whether to be pleased or annoyed that my father had asked Samir to look out for me. Local radio said that the IDF had occupied the whole of west Beirut and spoke of heroic resistance. I found the BBC World Service. They led on Grace Kelly, saying she'd died from her injuries. Then they spoke of Beirut and an IDF spokesman said that '2,000 PLO terrorists' remained in Beirut and they were determined to root them out.

Samir was back with my duffle-bag, throwing it onto the back seat.

'What now?' Samir asked.

'Let's go to the Commodore. Bob might know what's going on.'

We pulled onto Hamra Street to see Israeli soldiers crouching at street corners, nervously pointing their weapons everywhere. Most people seemed to be ignoring them, going about their business, mildly curious at the fact that yet more armed men were on the streets of Beirut, just in a different uniform.

'We were mentioned on the news, after Grace Kelly.'

'Which one is Grace Kelly?' he asked, slowing the car due to traffic.

'She was in that Hitchcock film, *Rear Window*. The one where he sees a murder from his window.'

'Why all this traffic? We've just been fucking invaded,' he said.

We didn't see the roadblock until we were caught in the queue for it, with cars behind us. I'd never seen Samir look concerned before. He put his hand to his door and I thought he was going to bolt, but he just wound down the window to let some air in. He searched for somewhere to turn off but we were stuck. He looked wild-eyed and it was making me scared.

'It's just an Israeli roadblock,' I told him, without much conviction.

'You're Lebanese and I'm Danish, right? We're just out for a nice drive, improving relations between our countries.' I checked my pocket for my passport, my armpits were wet.

'Are relations between our countries bad?' he asked. There were beads of sweat on his forehead.

'What's the worst thing that could happen?' I asked him.

'It depends on who is under there.' He pointed at the roadblock ahead, which was formed by two jeeps and an armoured personnel carrier. Next to the soldiers was a man in civilian clothing with a cloth sack over his head. Slits were cut in the hood for his eyes. He was looking into each car as it stopped at the roadblock. My heart was banging in my ears as we pulled another car ahead – now there were only two between us and the roadblock.

'I have a confession,' he said, looking straight ahead. Someone was being pulled from the back of a taxi and being made to go and sit with a group of three men who were crouched on the tarmac by the jeep, their hands clasped behind their heads.

I looked at Samir. 'Well?'

'I put your weapon in your bag, I thought it would be useful.'

'You stupid fucker.' If we were caught with the Tokarev we'd have no chance. 'Listen, maybe I should get out with the bag,' I said.

'And leave me on my own, you son of a dog?'

'If I could drive I'd let you go.'

'There's nothing to it, my friend. This is the clutch, this here is the gear. You need to depress the clutch …'

'Look! They're going.' The men sitting on the tarmac were being bundled into the back of one of the jeeps. The hooded informer got into the back of the other jeep with the other soldiers and they sped off. The half-track followed and the roadblock was gone. It all happened so quickly. The traffic started to move again.

'Were you afraid?' Samir asked, as he tried to light a cigarette with a shaking hand.

'Of course not – why, were you?' I helped him keep the lighter still. I wiped the sweat from my forehead. 'You put the fucking gun in the bag.'

'We could have taken them,' he said. He started laughing and shaking his head and I was laughing, laughing until I could taste tears. By the time we pulled up outside the Commodore I had a stitch in my side from laughing.

The lobby was full of news agency drivers, fixers, stringers and general hangers-on. We found Bob in the TeleNews edit suite, checking the morning rushes. On the screen Israeli tanks rumbled forward down the main Hamra Street followed by edgy-looking troops pointing their guns at the balconies above them. They were ignoring the bystanders, mainly women, standing with crossed arms as if watching a boring military parade. One elderly woman was shouting something at the passing tanks. Bob, looking drawn and tired, wanted a translation and I tried to make out what the woman was saying above the noise of the tanks.

'She says they're cowards to come in now that the fighters have left, that Beirut has had enough foreigners in it, that they should go home, that there's nothing left to destroy but women and children, etcetera, etcetera,' I told him. The woman wandered off shaking her head. Bob cracked open a cold beer and handed one to Samir. I shook my head when offered one.

'Have you managed to get into Sabra?' I asked him.

'No, it's closed off, none of the press has managed to get in.' He sipped his beer and looked for another tape in the pile on the editing desk. 'I'd like you to look at this footage,' he said, pulling out a tape and sticking it into the editing machine. 'I filmed it on the airport road this morning.' The small screen came to life and at first there were just Israeli Merkava tanks passing the camera on the coast road as they headed north. There were pictures of civilian cars passing, some shots of the planes overhead then back to the road, this time in a more built-up area. 'This is further north,' Bob explained as three truckloads of men in brand-new green uniforms passed the camera, waving and grinning at it. Bob stopped the film. Samir leant forward to look at the screen.

'They don't look like Israelis, and only a Lebanese who hadn't been in west Beirut this summer would behave like a monkey for the camera. But they don't have the markings of the Lebanese army.' He looked closer, asked Bob to forward the film frame by frame as the last truck passed the road and the camera swung round to follow its progress. 'Look. They don't have any markings.' The truck receded into the distance and the camera swivelled back. Samir leant forward again, jabbing the tiny screen. 'Stop it there. No, go back a bit.' The film froze, showing the wall of a house on the opposite side of the road, slightly blurred as the camera panned past it. 'Fuck their mothers. Look at that marking on the wall.' He stood up and started pacing the room, looking even paler than he had when we'd approached the Israeli roadblock. I leant forward to see which marking he meant among the spray-painted names of political parties and militias. But only one symbol was freshly painted on – a triangle within a circle.

'What does it mean?' Bob asked when I pointed it out.

'It's the Phalangist symbol,' I told him.

'So what? The whole of Beirut is plastered with militia logos.'

'This is in west Beirut, Bob. The Phalangists are hated here.' He slapped his forehead.

'Motherfuckers.' He turned to the editing desk and started fast-forwarding the footage, turning the dial to full speed. We were in a car heading back into Beirut, filming from the window. Stock footage, Bob said, useful for filler in the documentaries people would undoubtedly be making about this place. The camera passed walls pockmarked with bullet holes and covered in tattered and faded posters detailing the martyrs of various groups. He stopped the footage and there was the symbol again, freshly painted on the wall, with an arrow next to it pointing north. Again, he fast-forwarded, and again we stopped the film to reveal another triangle within a circle, with an arrow beside it. 'This is the route the trucks came,' he said. 'Now I wish I'd followed them.' We scanned through the video but saw nothing else of interest. We spun back to the last symbol and Samir pointed out that the arrow was pointing east down the Kuwaiti embassy road and that Bob would have carried on north on the coast road into Beirut proper.

'Where does that road lead?' Bob asked, but Samir was trying to get a cigarette from a new packet without much success.

'Towards the camp,' I told Bob, studying the symbol on the screen.

17

I was lying in bed in John's room at the AUB apartment, having been woken by a dawn chorus of birds. Samir and Fiona were in Asha's room, seemingly having patched things up. The previous night, over lamb kebabs and beer at the Commodore, Samir had given Bob a potted history of the Phalangists, albeit a simplistic version lacking the political context Faris might have provided. Fiona was there. She and Samir had arrived in sunglasses looking like international terrorists.

The Phalangists, Samir had told Bob, were Maronite Christians who thought themselves Phoenician in origin rather than Arab ('Who can blame them,' he said) and were set up by one Pierre Gemayel, father of Bashir killed not two days ago, who created his organisation after an inspiring visit to Hitler's Germany in the 1930s.

'And now they're allied with the Shlomos? How deliciously ironic.'

Samir shrugged, perhaps not knowing what he meant. He proceeded to tell Bob about what the Phalangists had done in the Lebanese Civil War. In 1976, at the height of the Civil War, the Phalangists had surrounded Tel al-Zaatar (translated as 'hill of thyme'), a large Palestinian refugee shanty town that happened to lie in east Beirut. That was another summer siege, Samir explained, and the camp was inevitably overrun and 3,000 people were killed. The camp was razed to the ground.

'They carved crosses on the bodies,' he added.

I'd explained that the Phalangists were looking for 'purity of race' in Lebanon, and were still determined to rid Lebanon of the Palestinians.

Lying in bed I recalled a poster commemorating the Tel al-Zaatar event that had little figures on it representing the number of people killed. There was nothing else on the poster, just the little figures with Tel al-Zaatar written across the top. Later that same year Palestinians retaliated with a similar, smaller-scale atrocity by evacuating and murdering the inhabitants of a Christian town south of Beirut where the survivors of Tel al-Zaatar were then housed. It so happened that my short military training had taken place on the outskirts of that small town. I'd gone with some boys from Sabra camp – rough kids compared to my schoolmates, who had their own cars and black servants. The military aspect of my training was nothing compared to what I learnt about people who had really been through it, even compared to the Sabra contingent. The other boys in the training camp were all orphans from Tel al-Zaatar, with no other prospects than to take up a Kalashnikov. The Sabra boys were God-fearing Muslims, unremarkable in a religion-obsessed country, although slightly at odds with the Marxist-Leninist youth group we were with. I was marked an outsider in several ways. One, I didn't believe in God, something I'd learnt to keep to myself due to the incredulous and hostile responses this information provoked at school. Two, I was half foreign and looked it, which meant that I was forever being asked things like 'What's "cunt" in Danish?' Three, I was the son of a cadre, which meant that some people there thought me worthy of special treatment. On the first day of training I was ushered by an instructor to the front of the food queue to fill my plate. Even now I cringed at the thought of it. I declined, determined to stand at the back of the line. At the confused response to this I worried that I'd committed a grave offence in the complex but unwritten rules of Arab etiquette. But the other boys appreciated the gesture, and it set the mood for the rest of the fortnight.

The Tel al-Zaatar orphans were crude, foul-mouthed boys and were the first Arabs I'd heard openly and constantly blaspheme in public. By the end of the first day the Sabra boys had gotten into a fight and by the end of the second day they'd had to be ferried back to the relative civilisation of Sabra camp to prevent a major confrontation. I, of course, stayed on and endured, because to leave would have caused my father considerable embarrassment. The fact that I stayed raised my standing even further. The blaspheming didn't bother me although the constant swearing became tiresome, especially as it was exclusively related to female sexual organs.

I wondered what had became of those boys, whether they'd been on the front line of the latest summer's siege, and what they would have said if they knew that the Phalangists were planning to finish what they'd started, this time knowing that there would be no resistance to speak of. I thought of Faris holed up in Sabra. I felt bad lying around reminiscing. There must be a way into the camp, I thought. I quickly pulled on my jeans and T-shirt and went looking for Samir and Fiona.

Samir had hard-boiled some eggs to rival the hospital kitchen's rubbery efforts. I outlined my plan to him and Fiona, which involved trying to get into the camp using the Red Crescent ambulance. Samir confirmed that he still had access to it.

'Won't they mind?' Fiona asked.

'I don't know – I won't ask them,' Samir said.

We discussed details but Fiona wasn't enthusiastic about going.

'We need a Western woman in the ambulance, particularly someone white like you,' Samir said.

Fiona pulled at her hair and said she would think about it. I told them I would try to convince Bob that smuggling him into the camp in the back of an ambulance was good for his career, although I doubted he'd need much persuasion. We agreed to meet at the Commodore later.

Najwa was still not at her apartment, which I was grateful for as it meant I didn't have to explain what I'd done with the passports. I did need to tell her about Lazy Eye though. I found a napkin in my jacket pocket from Samir's falafel place. I scribbled on it in English: 'Our old friend has made a surprise visit with some of his new friends', hoping she'd understand what I meant. I spent five minutes trying to get the napkin under the door without scrunching it up, and just as I succeeded the door opposite opened and an old woman stood there looking at me with undisguised hostility. I put on my best smile.

'You're always coming round here, you and that other man,' she said, pointing a crooked finger at me. I assumed she meant Abu Hisham. 'What do you want here?'

'She's a friend of my mother's,' I lied, although I wanted to ask her if it was any of her business. 'I'm just visiting. Have you seen her?' I asked.

'Do you think I watch her every coming and going?' I bet you do, I thought. She retreated into her apartment and slammed the door. I could see her beady eye glued to the peephole, where it probably was before she opened the door.

On Hamra Street Israeli soldiers were patrolling in a fairly relaxed style; there were even a couple of officers sitting at a pavement café. The other coffee drinkers eyed them with disdainful curiosity – an army who couldn't or wouldn't enter the city when it was full of fighters but now patrolled its streets as if victorious was no army in their view. Bob was in the editing suite, splicing together footage from yesterday. He showed me a video taken last night from the roof of the Commodore, which had been a favourite vantage point for filming F-16 raids during the summer. He'd filmed flares being fired over the south of the city, keeping whatever was underneath lit up like daytime.

'I'm pretty sure that's over the camps,' he said. I thought of Eli and the others stuck in the hospital, Faris somewhere in the camp. The flares kept a constant illumination going, but for what? Nothing good, that much was certain.

'I've got an idea on how we can get into the camp,' I said.

He looked at me. 'Go on.'

'We go in the back of an ambulance. Samir will drive it and Fiona will be the nurse up front. Well, she is actually a nurse.' I was talking too quickly but he was thinking about it. 'We'll travel in the back.'

'It's worth a try,' he said, but he wasn't exactly jumping up and down with excitement.

I told him Samir and Fiona would be at the hotel by lunch-time.

'As long as they don't pull up outside the hotel in an ambulance, otherwise we'll have every journalist in the place trying to get in.'

I said that I didn't think Samir was that stupid, but we gave each other a look.

The Commodore lobby was full of talk. Lebanese stringers told of people coming out of the camp and reports of terrible things going on, but it was difficult to distinguish fact from fiction in this volatile atmosphere and I knew that they were prone to exaggeration. This was true during the siege, when the official PLO version of events bore a proportional relation to the experience described. So fifty killed became a hundred, as if the truth wasn't bad enough. This stretching of the facts was probably a response to the lethargic reaction of the rest of the world to what was going on in Beirut. As Samir was fond of saying, 'What has to happen before people do anything?'

A Danish cameraman came in with his equipment, obviously straight from filming a story. Bob and he exchanged greetings and Bob introduced me. I got to speak my first bit of Danish since my mother left and it felt familiar and safe, like sitting in my grandmother's house in Skagen. I was filled with an urge to leave: walk out of the lobby into a taxi for the airport, get on a plane straight for Copenhagen, then get the train and ferry to Skagen. I could be there some time tomorrow if I left now, could register at Copenhagen University on Monday. Except the airport was closed and Eli was in the camp and Faris was missing and who knows what Youssef was doing. The Danish cameraman was telling us that he'd been refused entry into the camp but that he had some interesting film he wanted us to see.

So we were back in the TeleNews edit room where Bob stuck the Dane's tape into the machine and did a fast rewind.

'I filmed this after we were refused entry. It's a little bit shaky because I was using a telephoto lens.'

I listened to some technical talk between the two men as we first saw the Israeli checkpoint; the soldiers looking towards the camera, unsure as to whether to allow filming. An Arab voice off camera asked the camera man 'if he could see that' and the picture zoomed beyond the twitchy IDF to a military truck about a hundred metres behind them. It started to get wobbly then settled down but we could see a few civilian men sitting in the truck. An armed militiaman stood with them and some more men were being loaded in, pushed and pulled up as their hands were tied. The video blurred and the Dane explained that an Israeli soldier was walking towards the camera and that soon we'd lose the picture. I could see more people being loaded onto the truck and my heart stopped. But the truck was no longer visible and the screen was filled with the angry face of a blond soldier who was pointing his Galil at the camera.

'That's all there is,' the Dane said. I felt sick. I tried to turn the knob on the edit deck but my fingers were shaking.

'You look like you've seen a ghost,' Bob said.

I rewound the tape slowly, the Israeli soldier walked backwards and went out of focus. We could see the truck again and got five seconds of clear steady footage. I couldn't mistake his lanky frame even though I couldn't see his face. His hands were bound and he was being manhandled onto the truck. But when he sat down he was facing the camera and his long angular face looked towards the roadblock in resignation. It was Faris.

18

I saw Samir park his yellow taxi outside the Commodore and come in alone. I'd been waiting for him in the lobby after having a beer and a vodka in the bar with Bob, who was still there.

'Fiona's not coming. She doesn't want to get into trouble with her charity,' he said, his face twisted in disgust. He looked at me. 'When you don't need one you can't get rid of them, but when you do, they disappear.' He looked at me some more. 'What's the matter, my friend?'

'I need to show you something,' I said, getting up. Maybe it was a cowardly way to do it but I couldn't bear to tell him myself. Besides, he would have wanted to see the tape for himself.

I felt my throat constrict and my eyes burn as I watched Samir watch the tape. He was too calm afterwards. He lit a cigarette and looked out of the window onto the street below. We didn't speak for a while. Then he turned on his heels with a determined look on his face.

'Let's get Bob and go – the ambulance is in Fakhani,' he said.

Now we were racing down side streets towards Fakhani and Samir was completely focused on the road. Usually his driving was secondary to whatever else he was doing, like smoking or leering out of the window. I wished he would rage and swear or break something but the only clue to his anger was his fixed expression and the speed at which we were travelling. Bob was quiet in the back, fiddling with his equipment. As well as the Sony video camera he'd brought a Nikon for stills. In Fakhani we pulled into the municipal football stadium where Samir had killed the three-legged dog. It was less a stadium than a football pitch with a spectator stand. Samir parked beside a line of shrapnel-punctured cars. Among them I could see the ambulance with Red Crescent markings. I also noticed Samir's BMW 7 series and the UNICEF Nissan Patrol, both tucked behind the abandoned cars. For some reason, now that we were here, I felt nervous about taking the ambulance.

'Maybe we'd be better off in the Nissan,' I said. 'I mean since we don't have a nurse.' We looked at each other and Bob shrugged. Samir had adopted a blank expression.

'OK,' he said. I was worried that I was the only one concerned about doing this right but we piled into the jeep and Bob put his equipment in the back, under a canvas cover. It felt safe in the Nissan, its size and whiteness giving an illusion of invulnerability. Bob was in the front to give foreign respectability to our effort, although his ponytail was probably the same as having PRESS tattooed on his forehead. I was leaning forward between the seats, aware of my own breathing, trying to slow it down. Samir drove assertively at the Israeli roadblock, as if he was expecting to be waved through without stopping. The IDF had other ideas, however, and I could see them slipping off the safety on their Galils as we drew near. They were waving for us to turn back before we had even stopped. But we did stop and they surrounded the vehicle. Bob was shouting from the window.

'We need to go through – let us through please.' This was said in an authoritative voice designed to command respect. But all we got was a stream of Hebrew that didn't sound friendly. No one was able to speak English or Arabic. One of them got on a walkie-talkie and someone else signalled Samir to turn off the engine. We sat for a few minutes in an awkward silence, which was broken by the sound of a straining bulldozer working somewhere. It came into view, crossing the road on the other side of the roadblock. It was close enough that the noise made everyone turn and look and the militiaman driving it turned and waved at the roadblock. Nobody waved back. The bulldozer looked like one the Israelis used to flatten buildings in the south of Lebanon on their push north; it had been camouflaged and armoured for military use.

'Do you see that?' Bob asked. An IDF jeep pulled up beside us. A young soldier hopped out; he wasn't carrying a weapon. He spoke to the senior officer at the roadblock and approached the Nissan. I could see him looking in as he approached; his eyes met mine and I looked away.

'You can't come through here,' he said in Arabic, then again in English. He spoke as if by rote, like he couldn't care less. His Arabic was better than his English and I wondered where he was originally from. He looked drained and pale, as if he'd spent days and nights telling people they couldn't pass from one place to another.

'We're on official business,' Bob said.

The interpreter shook his head wearily. Samir was staring forward into the camp. I was worried that he was considering trying to drive through in a bid for martyrdom, taking Bob and me with him.

'It's no good,' said the IDF interpreter in Arabic. 'You cannot come through here. Go back. Go back before I tell them you are not UN.' He pointed his thumb behind him at the other soldiers. I translated this for Bob but Samir had already started the engine.

'What's going on in there?' Bob asked the soldier, but he'd turned away.

Samir put the car in gear and slammed on the accelerator. To my relief the Nissan jumped backwards at high speed, leaving rubber on the road in front of us. I thought Samir was just putting some distance between him and the roadblock so that he could build up enough speed to crash through it, but seeing his hand on the handbrake I warned Bob to hang on as Samir spun the jeep around, stopping only momentarily, and shifting into first before carrying on the right way forward. It was a manoeuvre he'd practised many times when bored, designed to get him out of trouble if needed.

Back at the stadium we transferred to the yellow Mercedes. I felt stupid for having suggested this fruitless exercise.

'Drop me off at the US embassy, Samir, I need to tell someone that something is fucking going on in there,' Bob said, pointing over his shoulder as we drove back towards Hamra.

The US embassy was a multi-storey compound on the seafront. The roof bristled with communications equipment, putting our own Signals unit in perspective. After dropping Bob off Samir stopped at a minor gate to the AUB. He just shrugged when I asked him where he was going. I barely had time to take my bag from the back seat before he accelerated away, leaving me standing in a darkening and empty street. I hadn't realised how late it was and the gate that Samir had dropped me off at was closed. I would have to walk round to the main gate to get in, which would mean passing near the apartment I had abandoned the day before, or the day before that, I no longer remembered. I decided to walk to the Etoile, where I hoped to find someone I could stay with.

The usual receptionist at the Etoile, an officious Lebanese with ideas incompatible with the two-star nature of the place, apparently no longer recognised me.

'Who are you visiting?' he asked in Arabic. I knew the bastard wouldn't challenge Faris or Samir in this way. My tactic was to play foreign and pretend I couldn't understand him. Hopefully he hadn't heard me speaking Arabic.

'I'm meeting someone in the bar,' I said in English, darting inside before he had a chance to remonstrate. It was empty apart from a small group at a table who didn't even look up when I came in. I sat at the bar and ordered a beer and some food, realising that I hadn't eaten all day. But they were no longer doing food, so I picked at some salted nuts instead. I felt uncomfortable sitting on my own. I would slip upstairs as soon as the receptionist had finished picking his teeth and decided to go and do something else. I heard an English voice at my side which I recognised immediately.

'Ivan? It is you, isn't it?' It was my English teacher, Mr Brampton, who had been teaching us right up until the first air raids this summer. He used to board at the school. He moved his bulk onto the stool beside me. He was still wearing his trademark linen suit and red cravat, perhaps unaware that he lived up to the image of the stereotypical Englishman. We shook hands. His fingers bulged unpleasantly.

'I didn't realise you were still in the country,' I said.

'I stayed on at the school for a bit because there were some boarders without anywhere to go, then I went over to east Beirut when things got too hot. Enjoyed the show from there.' He gestured towards the table he'd left. 'I've just come over to pick up some of my paraphernalia from the school and to visit friends.' I was surprised that I hadn't noticed him there when I came in. Maybe I just had too much going on in my life.

'Is the school still standing?' I asked. Thinking of its position on the south side of the city I imagined it must have been in the front line at some point.

'It's still there, but the Jew boys took it over and crapped in the new chemistry lab and headmaster's office. Shocking behaviour. I'd write to *The Times* about it if it would do any good.' He shook his head and I watched his jowls move. 'I couldn't believe that professional soldiers could behave that way.' He pursed his lips as if this was the worst outrage of the whole war. As if bombing and shelling civilians was all right but shitting in a school tipped the balance of unacceptable behaviour. He told me he was sailing to Cyprus the next day then flying to London. I told him I'd seen Emile and co. and that they were fulfilling their potential or destiny or whatever had been mapped out for them.

'In a cynical mood, I see,' he said. 'You never quite gelled with the others, did you?' He slid off his stool, then, perhaps appreciating for the first time that I was sitting in a hotel bar at night on my own with a duffle-bag by my side, put his hand on my shoulder.

'What are you doing here anyway – is everything hunky-dory, old chap?'

For a second I was tempted to unburden myself about everything that had happened to me: the siege, Black Thursday, the hospital injuries, the undercover stuff, being chased by informers, Faris being taken away in a truck, not knowing where to stay, not knowing what was happening in the camp. The feeling quickly disappeared, however, as I felt his fat fingers kneading my shoulder.

'Are you here with your family?'

The question was reasonable but the pitch in his voice had changed ever so slightly and his fingers dug a little harder into my shoulder. He'd never asked me about my family before. I looked at him, shook my head and he let go of my shoulder. Then the moment had passed and he was grinning and slapping me on the back. I wished him a good journey home. I turned to look at his companions as he headed back to the table. They were all Western males I'd never seen before.

I sipped my beer and considered whether to try Najwa's again or risk the AUB or go to the Commodore when the Norwegian anaesthetist walked into the lobby and looked into the bar. Although I couldn't remember her name I waved to her as if I was her long-lost son. She said she'd just come from doing a shift at a field hospital. I told her I needed somewhere to stay.

'Come up to the room,' she urged me.

I waved cheerfully to Brampton whose expression didn't hide his curiosity at me clutching my bag and leaving the bar with a woman three times my age.

I told her about Faris and she took my hands and looked into my eyes. We were sitting on Eli's bed and the concern in her face was enough to make me start crying. I tried to hide my face from her but she pulled me to her and hugged me, stroking the back of my head. She smelt of medicinal soap. When I was done I pulled back and she gave me a tissue.

'I feel terrible because Liv doesn't know about Faris,' I said. She looked at me, little wrinkles forming around her blue eyes.

'Maybe he'll be OK,' she said.

'No,' I told her, 'he won't be OK.'

She went into the bathroom. I lay down on Eli's bed. When she came back she pulled off my shoes while humming in a low voice. She turned off the main light and put on a reading lamp. I could see Eli's son staring out from the photo by my head. It felt reassuring to be on her bed. I could smell her musky jasmine perfume on the pillow. The anaesthetist's soft voice, cracked like the skin around her eyes, was singing a Norwegian lullaby. Its soporific effect had me drifting off into another, less troubled world.

But before I could let go of consciousness I heard a commotion in the hall, women's voices. I pulled my shoes on and we went to the door. There were two nurses outside the adjoining room, talking to some people we couldn't see inside. Apparently they'd been evacuated from a small hospital in the Shatila camp adjacent to Sabra. Removed by the Phalangist militia and handed over to the Israelis, they were ultimately given over to the Red Cross, who had driven them back to Hamra. The nurses talked of point-blank gunshot wounds and axe-blows being brought into the hospital that day. They told of the terror in the eyes of the Palestinian and Lebanese staff forced to stay behind. Their words were spoken quickly as if they needed to get their story out in a hurry.

'Have you spoken to the press?' asked the anaesthetist. 'People need to know what's going on.'

'We've just come from the Commodore,' said a white-faced English girl who didn't look much older than me. Then her voice went and she started crying and her companion led her away to her room.

'Is there any alcohol in here?' I asked, back in the room.

'Yes, I think Liv has something – but drinking is not going to help, Ivan.'

That's exactly what it's going to do, I thought. I found some Finnish vodka in Liv's bedside locker. I also found a picture stuck to the inside of the locker door. It was of her and Faris, taken – maybe even by me – on one of the evenings they were in my apartment. Faris was sitting on a chair laughing, cigarette in hand. Liv was on a cushion on the floor next to him, looking up at him with a quizzical smile. It looked like she'd just unintentionally made him laugh and didn't understand why. I took a slug straight from the bottle and showed the picture to the anaesthetist. She fetched a couple of plastic cups and I poured vodka into them.

'Beirut is not such a good place, I think,' she said, raising her cup to her lips.

'Maybe you're right.' I drank from my cup and held the vodka in my mouth until it burnt and I had to swallow.

19

When I woke I was in Eli's bed with my clothes on. My roommate was warm and pressed against my back, with her arm over me. She also had her clothes on. For a moment I had to think about what had happened during the night. I could see the near-empty Stolichnaya bottle on the bedside table, and I'd had enough of it to wonder at some point what it would be like to sleep with this woman, compared to Eli. She'd had enough to admit that she needed company, although I wasn't so far gone as not to understand that she didn't want sex. Her soft snoring didn't waver when I lifted her arm to go to the toilet; so I couldn't take credit for all the missing vodka. I drank lots of water from the tap then urinated the same amount, bracing myself against the bathroom wall. My urine was the colour of tea. She was still asleep as I let myself out. I never knew her name.

It had just gone 10.30 when I caught Bob getting into Samir's taxi outside the Commodore. He yelled for me to get in. Samir was in the driving seat, looking like he'd slept badly, in his clothes, and it was the first time I'd seen him with stubble. He didn't have his sunglasses on and the colour of his eye had moved into the dark end of the blue spectrum. He attempted a jovial greeting and drove slowly towards the camp as if he was in no hurry to get there. Bob filled me in on what he knew.

'A BBC journo has just come from the camp, things are worse than we thought. We'll see for ourselves,' he said, checking video stock and battery packs. He wouldn't tell me anything else.

Samir just shook his head when I asked him if he'd seen anyone. I watched the city move past my window, closing my eyes to my hangover and imagining that I was in my grandparents' car on the coast road from Skagen. Soon I would open my eyes and see sandy beaches and we would unload the car for a picnic on the dunes. When the car did stop, however, I opened my eyes and there were no dunes but just the dusty road outside the camp.

The Israeli roadblock we'd been stopped at the day before was gone; they'd regrouped further back up the road, huddled together outside the headquarters we'd just passed. I could see soldiers on the roof with binoculars. Perhaps they'd moved back to escape the smell coming from inside the camp. A sickly sweet smell that you get with old meat. It could have been coming from the bloated and decaying mule I could see lying stiffly on some fresh rubble. This rubble was everywhere on the perimeter, as if someone had started to make the camp smaller, working from the outside, then decided it was too big a job and given up. Bob had his camera on his shoulder. I carried his video pack. Another carload of journalists arrived. The Israelis looked on as we walked into the camp.

The smell inside was worse, you couldn't escape it by breathing through your mouth. You could taste it. I had to hold on to my stomach to stop from retching. How could one mule smell this bad? Then there was the noise. Although there were people, mainly elderly women, roaming the camp, the only noise was the buzzing, an underlying drone that I thought must be part of my hangover. We reached a stack of six or seven bodies in front of a destroyed house. The bodies were difficult to distinguish from the masonry as they were covered in the same dust and there'd been a half-hearted attempt to cover them with debris. Bob was filming and I was pulled towards them because I was attached to him through the video pack. As he got nearer he disturbed the flies, and the soundtrack to this scene became apparent as thousands of them took off from the wounds on the bodies, the pitch of their buzzing changing like a flock of birds suddenly taking flight. Although there were recognisable bullet wounds in the corpses, there were also gashes in the head, open wounds cleaved through flesh and bone into whatever was inside that I couldn't look at. Their wrists were swollen around the cord used to tie their hands together. Bob was saying something about them being lined up against the wall. I wanted to tell him about the English nurse in the Etoile the night before and her axe wounds but was afraid to open my mouth in case I vomited.

We moved on, letting the flies settle again. A woman rushed up to us begging and pleading for us to help her. She was pulling at Bob's sleeve, saying, 'They have taken my husband, help me find my husband.' Samir had to gently prise her off and she went over to the pile of bodies we had left and I watched her search the bloated and disfigured faces for her missing husband. Bob filmed her.

We moved on, following the sound of wailing. We came across elderly women, beating their chests and wailing inconsolably as they crouched beside a group of misshapen and mutilated bodies. Bob filmed them and we moved on, still on the main street, now seeing corpses everywhere and Samir stopped beside one, an old man in traditional ankle-length Arab dress. I recognised Donkey Man by the walking stick lying by him and the kufi that was knocked from his head, now split open, resting in a dusty pool of dried blood and brain matter. There were streaks of dried blood running down his cheeks. Samir pointed out that his eyes had been gouged out. I tried not to look at his eye sockets but didn't know where else to look.

Since there were no eyeballs in his head his eyelids were concave rather than convex.

'Why have they done that to his eyes?' I asked Samir.

'Because they are animals,' he said, as if I was stupid. I wanted to ask why they were animals but we were moving on. We came across a young woman who walked up to us. She looked calm and smiled at us. She could have been an aid worker or an Arab journalist, but she looked too young.

'Come, come,' she said in English. Not waiting for an answer she moved down an alley and we followed until she reached a one-storey breeze-block building. Outside lay a toddler on the ground by the wall. His head was caved in. She pointed at a blood stain on the wall above him.

'They smash his head against the wall,' she said. 'Again and again. By turn,' she said. Bob wasn't filming. 'He is my brother.' She led us into the house.

'My parents,' she said, in the same matter-of-fact voice, pointing to two slumped bodies on the floor of the living room. They had gaping wounds in their faces, fresher than the ones we had seen up until now.

'This is from last night,' she said, anticipating our question. She straightened the front of her dress. 'They did bad things to me,' she said in whispered Arabic. She glanced at her dead parents as if worried they could hear. She held up her fingers. 'Five men. Phalangists.'

Samir said nothing, though Bob wanted to know what she'd said.

'It doesn't matter,' said Samir, giving me a look of warning. I wished Asha were here, she would know what to do. We just stood there looking at the girl's dead parents. I was desperate to get out. The girl started to clear up, picking up crockery and clearing the table from what looked like the previous evening's meal. Samir asked her if she had other family in the camp, asked her her name. She shook her head. I was terrified that any second she would break down.

'Please don't tell anyone about what happened to me. Please,' she said to Samir in Arabic. She had a Lebanese accent. Tears began to stream down her face.

'Don't worry, sister,' Samir said.

I removed the video pack from my shoulder and left the house. Outside I tried to get as far away from the boy with the smashed head as I could before I knelt down and released the sparse contents of my stomach by the side of the footpath. When I was done I took involuntary deep breaths of putrid death, and vomited again. The others were standing beside me waiting.

Samir handed me a lit cigarette. 'Here, this helps with the smell.'

We moved on. There were more people on the street now and more wailing as relatives were found. People were coming out of their houses, they were talking to journalists. Bob now had the video pack and I was free to roam but I stuck with Samir.

'Shouldn't we send someone to help the girl?' I asked him as we moved down the street.

'Who can help her now?' he asked angrily, moving away, now holding a handkerchief to his nose. I looked round for Bob and saw him disappearing down an alley. I could see a hand poking out of some rubble next to me. The fingers were outstretched, as if waiting to catch a ball. I went down the alley I thought Bob had gone down, and the voices faded behind me as the alley got narrower.

'Bob?' I called, but all I got was the sound of flies. I passed another body lying on its side, hands and feet swollen round the cord that bound them. His trousers had been pulled down round his ankles. I swatted the flies from my face. There were doors either side but one was open further up.

'Bob?' I called into the gloom. I heard a movement inside but no answer – he probably didn't want voices on his soundtrack. On the other hand I didn't know how he could be filming in such darkness. I stepped inside and it was cool and the smell was not so bad, just sickly, like in surgery. Something scurried off into the other room. I waited for my eyes to grow accustomed to the dark; the only light was provided by a small window opposite the door. I was slippery with sweat. I made out a table in the middle of the room. My foot disturbed a bottle. I looked down to see an empty bottle of whisky. Something was discernible on the table and something, a form, on the floor. I heard a noise from the other room. I tried to call Bob's name but nothing came out of my mouth. It was round, the something on the table, the size of an elongated watermelon. The form on the floor, I could now see, was a body. The arms were stretched above the head and the clothes pulled over the face, a dark mass around the stomach and chest. My eyes flitted between the table and the body. My hand searched for the door frame behind me as I realised that I was standing directly in front of the door and blocking light into the room. I stepped to one side but my foot went into something soft and yielding. Instinctively I lifted my leg and lost my balance, stumbling forward onto the floor. On my knees I could see that it was a woman on the floor but that she had no breasts, not any more. She had a huge lateral wound in her stomach with lots of loose skin. I crawled backwards, feeling for the door opening with my feet. All I could think was that I mustn't vomit inside. I looked up onto the table and saw a tiny head, tiny hands and feet. I couldn't understand what had happened here, my eyes moved between stomach wound and small body, which looked like it was attached to the stomach wound on the body on the floor by a cord. I turned round and scrambled on my knees out of the house into the alley. My retching wracked my body and nothing came up but bile which mixed with my tears in the dust.

I was aware of screaming. 'They are coming back! They are coming back!' Maybe a man's voice, but in terror indistinguishable from a woman's. I got on my feet and ran down to the main street to see people scattering. Like everyone else, I was filled with terror. Even the journalists and Red Cross workers in face masks and gloves had been caught in the hysteria. I followed them as they ran back towards the Israeli position, but it turned out to be a false alarm. Bob was there and he'd found an IDF officer.

'Do you know what has happened in there?' he asked him.

The officer shrugged, no expression on his face. 'I just arrived today,' he said.

Bob started trembling. 'That's fucking crap. I saw you at a roadblock two days ago. You stopped me coming into the camp,' he shouted.

The officer was looking around for help but several journalists had gathered round, interested in the exchange. 'I don't know what's happening. I wasn't on duty.' His voice was high-pitched with panic. A general came up to the group, spoke to his officer in Hebrew. Another journalist, English, started asking the general when he knew, or suspected, what was going on in the camp.

'How could we know what was going on?' he said. 'We have not been in the camp.'

'You can smell what has been going on in the camp from here,' interjected Bob, his face red with anger.

The general smiled at Bob as if he was mentally ill and needed humouring. He raised his voice over the questions.

'Early this morning we helped some foreign workers to safety, once we realised they'd been held by the Phalangists,' he said. His deflection worked, some of the journalists seemed interested in this information. Fair-skinned people in trouble equated to front-page news at home. I looked to Samir but he was standing back, hadn't come up to the Israeli position. I realised that he'd never stood this close to an Israeli soldier. Perhaps he didn't trust himself.

'What about helping the locals?' said Bob, in a calmer voice, but his question was lost in a barrage of questions about the foreign workers. I gathered from the answers that they'd been handed over to the Red Cross after being evacuated from the hospital early that morning by the militia. I went back to tell Samir what I'd learnt.

'OK, let's go back and see if we can find them. We have to tell Liv about Faris,' he said.

I went and told Bob what we were doing. The general was winding up his impromptu press conference, refusing to answer questions about whether people were taken out of the camp in trucks, whether the Phalangists had used Israeli bulldozers, whether the Israelis had sanctioned what was going on.

'This is nothing to do with the IDF – this is an Arab-on-Arab problem,' he shouted, losing his cool and storming off. Bob and I went back to talk to Samir.

'I'll probably stay here and take some more footage – before someone clears it all up,' Bob said.

We walked back to the car so Bob could pick up the rest of his video stock and leave the tapes he'd filled. We were approached by the IDF interpreter we'd spoken to in Samir's UN jeep yesterday at the roadblock. Again he was unarmed and looked nervous. Up this close he didn't look much older than Samir.

'I knew you were not from the UN,' he said, smiling momentarily. We said nothing. 'They knew what was going on,' he said, pointing to the Israeli headquarters behind him by way of clarification. It was 'they', not 'we', I noticed.

'When did you know?' asked Bob.

'It was clear from day one.'

Bob went silent. His thing was pictures, not people, as he'd proved earlier, and I wished we had a print journalist with us who would know how to deal with this guy. Thankfully Bob was thinking the same thing.

'You should speak to my colleagues,' he said, pointing to some of the journalists gathered outside the Israeli headquarters. He started to take stuff out of the car. But it was as if the guy hadn't heard Bob.

'Do you know what happened in Chile, under Pinochet?' the interpreter asked.

'What?' Bob's annoyance was now showing in his voice.

'Where did most people disappear in Chile?' he persisted. Something clicked in my mind, something I'd read or seen or heard.

Bob looked at him, narrowing his eyes. 'Are you telling me they've taken people to the stadium?' Bob asked him. But someone was shouting 'Uri' from across the road and he looked behind us.

'I'm sorry, we are not allowed to talk to the press,' he said in a loud voice, completely changing his tone and moving round us.

'Fucking asshole,' Bob said.

20

Back at the Etoile by midday I was relieved to find Eli and Liv. They were both sitting on Eli's bed, sharing whatever vodka was left from the night before. My relief turned to anxiety when I remembered Faris. I didn't know whether they'd seen their roommate; part of me was hoping that they had. They looked exhausted and Eli had clearly been crying.

'Have you seen Faris this morning?' was the first thing Liv asked after I embraced both women. Samir was downstairs and I was going to have to do this alone. I shook my head, telling her I'd just come from the camp. Before I could elaborate Liv launched into a description of their morning: some militia had come into the hospital early on and asked for all the staff to congregate outside for interrogation. They'd made them walk down Sabra main street in single file. Gunmen lined the street. A Palestinian doctor tried to leave with them but had been taken out of the group and they'd heard shots. Some of the buildings had been bulldozed and they passed bodies on the ground. Liv was spitting this out as she paced up and down, like she was trying to get rid of some foul-tasting thing in her mouth. I lit her a cigarette, which she took without acknowledgement.

'Was Youssef there when you left?' I asked Eli. But she was looking somewhere else.

Liv stopped pacing. 'I think so, everything happened so quickly,' she said.

'They lined us up against a wall,' Eli said. She took a breath. 'They pretended to shoot us – called us Baader-Meinhof, communists.'

'All good things,' said Liv, putting her hand on Eli's head and blowing smoke out in thin streams from her nostrils. I sat next to Eli and put my arm round her. She'd started to shake, the shock of the mock execution hitting her in the retelling.

'I've never been so glad to see Zionists,' said Liv, resuming her pacing. 'The Israelis took us to their headquarters and handed us to the Red Cross, after showing us how they were treating some of the wounded from the camp.' She snorted to indicate her disdain of this public relations effort and squatted in front of me on the bed, putting her hands on my knees.

'Enough about us. Tell us, what's the situation in the camp?' Her face was full of concern. I wanted to tell them what I'd seen: the bodies in the street, the ones buried under the rubble, the mutilations, the children, the rape, the eviscerations. I didn't know how to tell it or where to begin. Besides, I had Faris to deal with first.

'It's bad,' was all I could say before taking the vodka bottle from Liv and putting it to my lips. The rawness helped with the smell from the camp that still clung to the back of my throat. 'There's something else that I need to tell you first though,' I said, putting the bottle down and taking her hands to stop mine from shaking.

In a makeshift press room at the Commodore Asha and John were talking to journalists, telling an expanded version of the story Liv had told me. Samir had just dropped Liv and me off, leaving Eli to sleep in her room. Liv was remarkably calm on hearing about Faris and had been talking through a plan which involved taking someone with clout to the national stadium in the hope that that was where Faris had been taken for questioning. To my shame I'd not considered the possibility that we could do something to find him. She, however, was assuming that he was still alive.

Samir had held on to me as I was getting out of the car. 'Tell her she's wasting her time,' he said in Arabic. 'But in a nice way, like you know how,' he'd added.

Now, once the journalists realised that they weren't learning anything new from Asha and John, they started to drift away. I went up to them both as they got up from the table that was acting as a rostrum. Although pleased to see me they looked confused, unsure of what they were supposed to be doing next. John wanted to go to the British embassy, to report what had happened. They were pale and had dark rings under their eyes. Asha was pulling at a stray wisp of black hair. I told them about Faris and Liv's plan to go to the stadium.

Asha shook her head, put her hands to her face. 'Is there anything else that can happen in this place?' she said through her fingers. She took her hands from her face and looked at John. 'I need to get back to the hospital,' she said.

'The hospital will be fine without you for a few hours,' John said. 'There are plenty of people who've been resting up for the last three days who are already on their way. You need to get some rest. Can you get to the AUB?'

Asha nodded but then shook her head. 'I'd rather come with you to the embassy,' she said.

Liv approached us and she and Asha hugged. I could see Liv holding back her tears. John gave her a pat on the back.

'I've found a Norwegian journalist who will go to the stadium with me. Maybe we can speak to someone in charge there,' she said.

'Do you even know Faris's full name – or that Faris is his real name?' John asked.

Liv shook her head. 'I have this,' she said, taking something out of her back pocket and handing it to John. It was the photo of her and Faris I'd found in her bedside locker, taken in my apartment. John looked at it and handed it back. I could see he was struggling for something good to say.

'I hope you find him.'

Liv nodded. Her mouth was set rigid, like if she let it slacken the rest of her would follow. She put the photo back in her pocket.

'I'll come with you,' I said, without thinking. I wanted to believe that there was a chance that Faris was alive, that maybe he'd just been taken away for questioning. I felt a need to do something, anything, to gain control of even a small part of what was going on around me.

'Thanks, Ivan, but you've seen enough today,' Liv said, smiling and shaking her head in a way that meant she didn't want me to press it further. She went off to find her Norwegian. Bob came into the lobby with some other journalists and he waved at me and headed over.

'Was Youssef at the hospital when you left?' I asked Asha.

She nodded and Bob appeared at our side, smelling of the camp.

'You guys have just come from the camp, right?' asked Bob.

'Like we told the others, go and see for yourself,' John said, his face hard.

'He's OK. I know him,' I said.

'Did you see what happened?' Bob asked them.

'We were in the hospital,' Asha said. 'We only became aware that something was going on when the place started swarming with people thinking it was a safe place to be.'

'Plus of course the types of injuries we were getting through the door,' John added.

'So you don't know what actually happened in the camp?' Bob asked.

'Only what I've heard, and what we saw when we were escorted out,' John said. 'I know how people can blow things out of proportion here.' He looked at me. 'No offence intended, pal.'

I shrugged.

'You couldn't exaggerate this stuff,' Bob said. 'Why don't you come and see for yourself?' He patted his video pack.

Back in his editing room we sat round the screens. I steeled myself to relive the morning's sights.

We went past the bloated mule, then up close to the pile of bodies with their wrists swollen over their bonds. The smell hit me again as the flies took off. I couldn't get it out of my nostrils.

'They must have been dead two days given the state of the bodies and the heat,' said John. 'Which means they were killed on Thursday.' We moved on to the body of Donkey Man and this time I noticed that his right fist was clenched and bent back in an unnatural shape and wondered whether he'd tried to stop his killers.

'It's Donkey Man,' Asha whispered.

I lit a cigarette to kill the smell. There were more bodies against walls. Bob had managed to pick out where bodies had been incorporated into rubble by bulldozers.

'My problem is that none of it is fucking broadcastable – I'm going to have trouble finding something acceptable to show to our dinner-time demographic back home,' he said, smiling grimly to himself. We got to new footage that he'd taken after Samir and I had left and there were people now sitting over their dead relatives, weeping and pulling their hair or wandering around in a daze, screaming at the growing comprehension of what had happened.

Cut to a six- or seven-year-old girl, her limbs stiffened and raised off the ground in a bizarre way that showed there was no rest even in death. Her chest was bare and a cross had been slashed into it. Cut to a tiny garden where two mature women lay side by side, face down on some rubble from which a baby's head stuck out.

'Its eyes are still open,' John said in a wavering voice.

Cut to a woman crying to the camera, carrying the body of her dead child, still limp and with a large chunk of its head missing. She's offering the boy up to the camera and Bob flinches in his seat as if he was there again. Now she's talking to the camera. I translated without taking my eyes off the screen.

'Apparently she begged them to spare her five-year-old son but they said he would grow up to be a terrorist so they shot him in the head.'

The screen went blurry but I realised it wasn't the screen. Cut to a small body with detached limbs, like a dismembered doll, the arms and legs arranged on the torso in the shape of a cross, the stumps cauterised with flies. Then it was dark inside a house and I was worried and relieved at the same time that this was the same house I went into, but it wasn't. It was a man tied to a chair, his face mutilated beyond recognition. I could only tell it was a man because his disfigured genitals were exposed. The camera moved round the room to where a woman was sitting on the floor with a child in her lap. They'd both been shot in the head. We were back in daylight and Bob had focused on a prone body, lying restful in the recovery position, but a close-up revealed a grenade beneath it, ready to go off if someone dared to move it. The tape ended and Bob said he had further material.

'I can't see any more, please,' said Asha.

John stood up. I got up too.

'I think we'll leave you to find something usable from that lot,' John said.

Later on that evening I stood under the hot shower in Asha's AUB apartment, trying to get rid of that smell which seemed to have lodged in my pores. I sluiced water up my nostrils, in my ears. Samir, Asha, John, Eli and Liv were in the apartment and I could smell onions frying, reminding me that I hadn't eaten all day. Everyone else had showered and Asha had put the washing machine on twice on a hot cycle.

I came out wrapped in a towel to find Eli and John in the living room. Eli was in men's clothes that were too big for her. She patted the sofa beside her. I sank into the cushion next to her and watched John, wearing a traditional jallabiyah he'd found, trying to pick a record from the large collection. I could hear Asha arguing with Samir in the kitchen about how the onions should be chopped. I took Eli's glass from her hand and enjoyed the burning whisky at the back of my throat, the warmth flowing through my veins. I pressed my thigh against Eli's. She pressed back.

'Chopin or Bach?' John asked me, holding up two records. I told him that it didn't matter, that I didn't care.

'Sounds like you need Bach,' he said, putting the Chopin back and carefully taking out the vinyl from its cover. I was about to ask where Liv was when she appeared in the doorway. Eli tensed beside me and grabbed my leg. Liv was holding the Tokarev in her hands, down between her thighs. She must have found it in my duffle-bag in the bedroom. Her hair was wet and she was in just a T-shirt. The gun looked huge in her hands. I couldn't see if the safety was on. Her eyes were bright and she was swaying on her feet.

'What are you going to do with that?' Samir said, laughing from the kitchen door. He started to move forward but Asha held him back.

'I never thought I could use one of these. I've never wanted to before,' Liv said. She lifted up the gun to examine it more closely. Her thumb was covering the safety catch.

'It isn't the answer,' Asha said in a soft voice, moving in front of Samir. I could hear something frying in the kitchen, I could smell the onions. Samir went back through the door and the sound faded. Eli said something in Norwegian which I couldn't understand but Liv just shook her head.

'Is it loaded?' Samir asked me in Arabic.

'I can't remember,' I said.

Liv's eyes flitted between us as we spoke.

'You know it's rude to speak Arabic in front of people who can't understand you. Faris would never do that,' she said.

'You're upset,' said Asha in her soft voice. 'We're all upset about Faris, but you are especially of course.' She stepped forward but Liv stepped back, keeping the distance between them.

I felt stupid sitting on the sofa wrapped in a towel but didn't want to get up too suddenly.

'Don't be such a fucking drama queen, lassie,' John said in a loud voice. He'd just finished cleaning the record with the special duster and was carefully placing it on the turntable. All of us, including Liv, looked in his direction. 'This crap is going to help no one – we've got to cope with this thing in our own ways – but we've got to keep it together as well.' He pointed at Asha. 'Now she has God, a lost cause as far as I'm bloody concerned given what's happened, but the rest of us have to find some other way of coping with this shit.'

I looked at Asha but she was looking at Liv who was studying John through red eyes. He must have looked ridiculous to her in his traditional peasant dress, similar to the outfit Donkey Man was wearing when he was butchered. He smiled at her. 'Surely your Communist Manifesto has something to cover this sort of thing?' he said. 'Chapter four, section three: when the ruling class uses one section of the proletariat to subdue another, or something along those lines.' He was chuckling to himself. I saw Liv's mouth twitch but something had changed in the way she was holding the gun, like she didn't know what to do with it.

'It doesn't deal with the reality of all', gesturing with the gun, 'this ...' Her voice sounded like it had been sapped of life.

Asha stepped forward and put one hand on Liv's shoulder and the other on the gun and Liv was letting it go. Eli stood up. Asha handed the Tokarev to Samir by the trigger guard as if it carried a virus.

'Get rid of it,' she spat.

He took it from her and Asha and Eli led Liv, now crying and shaking, back into the bedroom. Samir sat down next to me on the sofa and started to unload the automatic.

Asha came back in. She didn't look at me or Samir.

'John, do you have something in your black bag to help Liv?'

'If I had something that would help I would be taking it myself, or giving it to the survivors in the camp.'

'This isn't the time to be funny, John,' Asha said sharply.

John rolled his eyes at me and looked for his doctor's bag. The Bach started to come through the speakers. When they'd both gone into the bedroom Samir tapped the side of his head.

'These foreigners are crazy,' he said.

21

The following morning we were driving back to the camp in Samir's car. Liv had had no luck in finding Faris at the national stadium – the IDF had refused all entry – but had learnt from the relatives amassed outside that some people had been transported from there in trucks. Samir had heard that trucks with prisoners had been seen passing through the Christian villages beyond east Beirut. None of this was good news.

Eli had protested at being left behind with Liv but not too forcefully; part of her was relieved not to be going back to the camp, and besides, Liv couldn't be left alone as she was still medicated. I wasn't that keen to go back myself but wanted to make sure Youssef was OK. Now, as we approached the camp again I could see the Lebanese army were in place and that the IDF were nowhere to be seen. Apparently they'd retreated to the airport, probably hoping that distance from the camp would weaken their association with what had gone on. When we arrived the camp was full of post-massacre activity. Journalists, aid workers, relatives, diplomats, politicians and the curious all moved among the dead. Bodies had been lined up in rows and were being buried in a large trench dug by a bulldozer. Asha was livid when she saw this from the car.

'They're burying all the evidence,' she said, trying to escape the car before it had even stopped. As she opened the door the heat and smell grabbed me by the throat; it was sweeter and sicklier than the day before. Most of the Red Cross and Red Crescent workers had masks on. Samir preferred chain-smoking as a way to cover the smell and I took his lead, determined not to throw up again. Asha found a Lebanese army officer to march up to, with me trotting behind. The officer was surprised at Asha's claim that she'd been in the camp hospital when all this was happening.

'He asked why anyone would want to be here that didn't need to be,' I translated.

'Because we are – or were – trying to help these people, tell him,' she said, but I shook my head, knowing that this would be met with equal disbelief.

'I don't think he considers that necessary,' I told her, hoping she'd drop it. She looked at me in despair and strode off in small steps, finding a foreign-looking worker in a Red Cross vest.

'Is someone counting the dead and cataloguing the type of injuries?' she asked him, not even bothering to introduce herself. He looked flustered and hot; his mask was hanging from one ear, obviously ineffective against the smell.

'We are trying to prevent a health hazard,' he said in a French accent. 'And the Lebanese army want everything cleared up quickly.'

'I bet they do,' said Asha.

The Frenchman moved away to supervise two people who were having trouble getting a body into the ditch in one piece. They kept having to pick pieces of it up and put them back in the blanket. I glanced down at the line of bodies I had tried to avoid looking at. Mercifully they were covered in sheets. Survivors, mostly women, moved down the line, trying to find missing relatives. Luckily there was too much activity for the flies to settle but, when the women lifted back the sheets to check the faces, I could see that they'd been left with a legacy of maggots. John suggested we head for the hospital. I hoped to find Youssef there.

John and Asha went into the hospital ahead of me as I finished my cigarette with Samir. We watched people carrying their belongings, either coming back or leaving, it was impossible to tell. Some of them would be refugees for the second, third or fourth time.

The lobby was empty. I worked upwards floor by floor but I couldn't find Youssef on the children's ward and the orthopaedic ward had just one body in it, covered by a sheet, the head end bloodstained. I noted with relief that it was an adult-sized body. I moved up a floor and found activity in the Intensive Care ward, where it looked as if all the remaining patients had been placed. Asha was there with John and they were getting status reports from the medical staff, none of whom I recognised. The Egyptian doctor who used to run the ward wasn't there, and most of the people who were, even the nurses, were foreign. They were confused about where the rest of the patients had been taken. I was now getting worried about Youssef's whereabouts.

An Italian doctor was talking to John in broken English. Asha was examining patients, greeting them like old friends.

'Yes, some of the patients were removed by the Phalange after you left,' said the Italian. 'Some went home on their own and the badly injured were taken to another hospital by the Red Cross.' No, he didn't know where they were all taken. I told them about the inhabitant on the orthopaedic ward.

'I haven't had time to move him – they are telling me he was shot in his bed by the Phalange,' said the doctor, waving his hand dismissively: a patient murdered in his bed was the last thing he needed to worry about. I left Asha and John to do whatever they had to do and found Samir on the street, lighting one cigarette with the end of another.

'Youssef is gone,' I told him.

'He's probably back home,' Samir said, slapping the dust off his shoes with a handkerchief. I looked at him but he ignored me. I looked at him some more. 'Damn your father, you want to go searching for him, don't you?' He ground his cigarette butt with his heel.

'We've got to do something, Samir. We have to rescue something from this ...' I waved my hands.

'I know I said I'd look out for you, but chasing camp kids is not something I thought we'd be doing. Do you even know where he lives?'

I shook my head. 'I know his family name though, and I know he lived with his aunt.'

'OK, OK, let's see if we can find the little son of a bitch.'

Several questions later and we were knocking on the iron door of a small house with shrapnel holes in the outside wall. It swung open and my heart started to thump.

'Wait here,' Samir said. I didn't object as he disappeared inside alone. I lit a cigarette and watched an elderly couple wheel their belongings down the street on a barrow. A scrawny cat sat on the front acting as look-out. Samir came out, white-faced. He took deep breaths and leant against the wall. I gave him my cigarette.

'Tell me the worst,' I said.

'The good news is that Youssef isn't there ...' He took a drag. 'The bad news is that his aunt is.'

'Shit, shit, shit. Maybe he was taken to another hospital by the Red Cross?'

'We're wasting our time,' Samir said.

I looked at him. 'I need to know,' I said.

He sighed and rolled his eyes, shook his head.

'I need to know,' I said.

Two hours later we were parked outside our third hospital.

'This is the last place we try,' he said. 'This time you're on your own. I'm sick of hospitals.'

I left him trying to find music on the radio.

This place was huge and bustling. Near the Green Line, it was a Lebanese government-run institution that didn't smell of disinfectant like the camp hospital. Nobody stopped me as I walked from ward to ward, past beds full of people surrounded by relatives. I eventually came to a set of closed double doors behind which I could hear the sound of children laughing and shrieking. Inside it smelt of piss and shit. Cots with bars lined the walls – cots in which naked children of various ages were lying, either in a foetal position or flat on their backs, staring at the ceiling. They all had shaven heads. One of them had climbed out of his cot and was laughing and jumping around, banging on the cot of his neighbour, who was looking out through the bars with a stupid grin on his face. The escapee kid's left wrist was tied to his cot with a torn-up sheet. Looking again I saw that all the children were constrained in the same way. They yelled and shrieked when they saw me, some of them jumping up and down. A man in a white jacket and shaven head was sitting in a chair at the opposite side of the room to the door. He was reading a newspaper which he put down, annoyed at being disturbed. He didn't get up. He had to shout over the din.

'What do you want?'

'Children's orthopaedic ward.' He pointed to the ceiling. On the other side of the doors I stopped to take a deep breath, tried to focus on why I was there.

The ward upstairs was a mixed orthopaedic ward, with no distinction between adults and children. I walked between the rows of beds on either side but there was no sign of Youssef. I noticed a balcony at the far end, on which there were several patients smoking. A small boy in an oversized wheelchair, his back to me, had his hands on the railing, looking down the five floors to whatever was there. His injured leg was on the floor, the bandage dirty and rust-coloured with dried blood. I could see a large spotting of fresh red at the heel. I went to the balcony door. My knees weakened as I stepped out onto the narrow space. I called but he didn't hear me. I moved closer, my stomach lurching as Youssef put his head over the railing to get a better look below.

'When's the last time you tried your crutches, boy?' I said, in an official-sounding voice. He swung his head round, his dirty face beaming at me, then he caught himself and scowled.

'Where have you been, you shit?' he said, his mouth trembling.

I couldn't help smiling some more.

'Let's get out of here,' I said, bending to lift him from the chair, keeping my eyes off the railing. He put his arms round my neck and I lifted him by his skinny legs. His face crumpled and he buried it in my neck. I had never heard him cry before, except when in pain, but that was different to this sobbing. I moved into the ward. A doctor, changing a dressing, shouted to me as I passed him but I looked straight ahead, pretending I hadn't heard. Then another doctor stood in my way as I walked towards the entrance, my neck wet with Youssef's tears.

'You, where are you going with the boy?' he said.

I stopped. 'It's OK,' I said, stepping round him, 'I'm his brother.'

Back in the outpatient clinic in Sabra Hospital Asha changed Youssef's dressing, the smell of which Samir had complained about all the way back in the car. Youssef swore and grimaced as the last bits of gauze came off, stuck as they were to his wound. Asha called John in and they peered and prodded at his foot. I concentrated on looking at Youssef's face. A sweat had broken out on his forehead.

'Is my aunt dead?' he asked, as if asking the time.

I nodded. He winced but it was from physical pain. I heard John say he was going to inject a local anaesthetic.

'What happened here yesterday?' I asked, partly to distract him.

'Yesterday they came for us – yesterday morning.' He yelped at the needle going into his tender flesh. 'After the doctors left, the Phalangists came round the beds and removed some of the men. They killed some others in their beds.'

I ignored the digging that was going on at the other end; Asha was saying something about the need for reconstructive surgery.

'Then what happened?'

'The Red Cross took some of us away to the other hospitals is what happened.' He looked at what they were doing to his foot. 'That girl with the missing leg is lucky – she went to England before all this happened.'

'Yes, I'd forgotten about her.' They'd gone with the BBC team only the day before the camp was sealed off.

'The interpreter went too, you know,' he said. He looked at me as if he and I were stuck here through some negligence on my part. Bloody swabs dropped at my feet.

'They say it rains all the time in London,' I told him. He frowned with pain.

'Is that the worst thing you can say about it?' he asked.

Back at the Etoile Eli was delighted to see Youssef again.

'I'm so glad you found him,' she said. She bent over to give him a hug and a kiss in his oversized wheelchair. He squirmed at this attention but I saw him trying to get a good eyeful of cleavage and he managed to get his hands on her waist. He winked at me when he saw me glaring at him. The news of his aunt had possibly not sunk in or, in light of what else had happened, he couldn't process it. Asha wanted Youssef to stay at the hotel but the hotel manager wouldn't hear of it. Perhaps he thought having a wounded boy staying would put off the tourists. I readied myself to translate a fight between him and Asha but she just shrugged and said she'd take him to the AUB until things stabilised in the camp. John took the wheelchair and they got ready to go.

'Are you going too?' Eli said, touching my arm. Asha and John were standing behind Youssef, looking at me as if I was a wayward son.

'I'll catch up with you,' I told them.

'We'll expect you for dinner,' Asha said. I headed upstairs behind Eli before Youssef made some lewd comment.

Her room was empty.

'Where's Liv?' I asked.

'She's at the embassy, organising the trip back.' Eli sat on the end of her bed and patted the mattress beside her. Close up she smelt clean, which made me aware of my own dirty state; I stunk of post-massacre camp and unclean hospitals. I put my hand on her knee.

'When's she leaving?' I asked, moving my hand up her thigh. She took my hand and held it in hers.

'We're both leaving together,' she said.

I removed my hand and rubbed between my eyes. I stood up.

'When?' I asked.

'Maybe tomorrow – probably tomorrow, if Liv can organise it.' She patted the bed beside her again but I moved to the window. I could see Asha, John and Youssef move down the road in the distance. They looked like a family together. I now wished I'd gone with them.

'But the airport is still closed,' I said, hating my petulant tone.

'We're going through east Beirut, getting a boat to Cyprus. That's what Liv has gone to the embassy for, to get them to drive us to the port.'

'Then tonight is our last night.'

She crossed her legs and my chest constricted; it was like she was closing a door. I watched her, thinking of what to say.

'I'm going home to my partner, Ivan.' I winced at her manner; that of an adult explaining something to a difficult child. 'I'll be seeing him tomorrow or the day after. I don't think anything will happen tonight.'

I was trying to keep quiet, telling myself that keeping quiet was the right thing to do, the manly thing to do. 'That's not what I mean. I mean just sleeping together. Next to each other. Like we used to before we, you know. I mean, what's changed?'

She shook her head and smiled, raised her eyebrows at what I was saying. I found her smile patronising.

'Everything has changed,' she said.

I looked out of the window again but Asha, John and Youssef had disappeared from view.

I arrived at the AUB apartment in time for dinner. We sat outside even though the evenings were a little colder now. Youssef was shiny from being scrubbed clean, John joking about how he'd had to run two baths before the water ran clear, how they'd rigged a sling over the bath to keep his foot dry. I picked at Asha's lentil dhal. Youssef complained about the food; he'd not had curry before. I let him eat my rice while Asha fried him a couple of eggs.

Samir turned up after dinner, ashen-faced with tiredness. He refused to even sit down, saying that he couldn't stay long. Youssef and I were alone outside, he with huge earphones clamped to his head, nodding in time to whatever John had put on. Samir ruffled Youssef's hair but he pushed Samir's hand away, annoyed.

'Did you tell him about his aunt?'

'He'd already guessed.'

Samir was going to touch Youssef's head again but thought better of it.

'I was hoping Liv was still here,' he said, picking at leftovers on the table.

I told him that she was at the Etoile with Eli.

'So why aren't you there? Aren't they leaving tomorrow?'

I mumbled something about having already said goodbye; if you could count our hug and her plea for me to do something with my life a goodbye. It had been more like seeing off an anxious aunt.

Samir looked at me and shook his head. 'You ever become a man with her, my friend?' he asked in Arabic.

'Is that how you become a man?' I asked.

He picked up a piece of bread and rolled it between his hands until it was a doughy ball. 'I've been to see Faris's family. I wanted to let Liv know that he'd told them about her.'

'He had family?' I asked.

'Of course. Do you think he was created from dust?' He moved to the living room where no doubt he thought he could have a more intelligent conversation. Asha was wondering aloud whether the massacre would be a turning point for the Palestinians, whether the world would do something to tackle the problem. John just shrugged his shoulders, swirling whisky around in his glass. It was Samir that spoke.

'It wasn't just Palestinians killed in the camp, it was Lebanese too. Maybe 25 per cent of them, maybe more, but we'll never know.

They were only poor uneducated Lebanese, so no one will worry.' He stopped, aware now that we were all looking at him, then continued. 'It's the same for the Palestinians. Do you think any educated or rich Palestinians died in the camp? Do you think any PLO cadres were there? No, only Faris and his friends were stupid enough to be there.'

I'd never seen Samir so worked up.

'It's always the way,' said John.

'I have to believe this will change things – we have to have hope for the future,' said Asha.

Samir snorted angrily. 'I like you and I salute you for being here,' he said, saluting. 'But you are being like a child. This will change nothing except maybe some headlines for a few weeks.'

I wanted to agree with Asha but Samir had history on his side.

'Then Faris is gone for no reason,' she said harshly.

'Faris is gone, probably dead, because he tried to defend the camp; he wanted to do the right thing which was the stupid thing. But he has wasted his life for nothing, the camp could not be defended by such a small number of fighters. It was a foolish gesture.'

To me, Faris was a hero and a martyr, words that I felt had been devalued over the years by too many deaths. Faris was someone who I could only hope to look up to rather than aspire to be like.

'Faris was a hero,' I said, blushing. 'Because he did the only thing he knew, which was to try and defend those people.'

Samir left, after hugging Asha, and we went to bed. Youssef and John were sharing his room while Asha was in the main bedroom and I was on the sofa. I could hear Youssef snoring as soon as he put his head down but I couldn't sleep despite the exhaustion that infused my body. I was trying to stop images from the day before coming into my head, trying not to see the small shape on the table connected to the body on the floor. To counter them I tried to think of Eli and our afternoon together in the apartment but things got confused in my head. First Eli naked in the bed, then the girl straightening her dress in her house in the camp, with her dead parents in the room and her dead brother outside, telling us that she'd been raped. I gave up and went out to the balcony. I was surprised to see John there, smoking a cigarette. I'd never seen him smoke before, except for hashish. I sat opposite him and removed a cigarette from the soft packet like I'd seen Faris do, by tapping the bottom. We looked out over the Mediterranean sea, illuminated by a full moon. I was just in my underwear and a T-shirt and goose pimples were forming on my legs. The cold helped to repress my thoughts.

'Can't sleep either?' he asked eventually.

I shook my head. We watched a car travel down the Corniche, its headlights picking out palm trees in the central reservation.

'Will they ever go away, do you think? The images, I mean, and the smell ...' I said.

He shook his head. 'I don't think so, laddie. No, I don't see how they can.'

22

A week after Eli had gone home I opened her letter for the second time. I was in the sitting room of my apartment, the table covered in empty wine, beer and vodka bottles. The first time I'd opened it was the night before, when it was handed to me by Lene, a medical technician fresh off the plane from Oslo. The first thing I'd seen on opening it was the money and the photograph, which I had left in the envelope, not wanting to take them out in front of the others. Lene was here for two weeks to instruct the locals in the use of some new intensive-care monitoring equipment that had been donated by the Norwegian government. I had left her sleeping in my bed. I counted $500 and put it in my wallet. I pulled out the letter and the photograph fell from it. It was of Eli and me taken in this room. We were sitting next to each other on the sofa with our glasses raised to the photographer who must have been sitting where I was now. We were smiling, our shoulders touching because we'd been asked to move together so we would be in frame. On the back she'd written, 'The first night we met.'

Her one-page letter was addressed to 'My Beautiful Boy' and said the same things that it had said the last time I read it. Liv was going to Nicaragua, where apparently the Sandinistas were in control, an actual people's revolution had happened, according to Liv. The money was to 'get out of Beirut and do something with your life, to fulfil your potential'. Also, Lene was 'very nice' and I should make her feel at home, like I had Eli. I read the letter again, but could find nothing beyond the kind and concerned tone. I didn't know what I was looking for – a declaration of love, perhaps, an emotional outpouring of regret at leaving Beirut. Lene had told me that Eli had asked her to look after me and last night, when the others had gone, she'd done just that. I wasn't sure whether it was what Eli'd had in mind. When I joked with Lene about it afterwards she'd said, in all seriousness, 'But ja, of course it is.' And maybe it was what Eli had wanted – to put herself out of my mind by putting someone else in my bed. But Lene wasn't Eli, far from it. She was younger – only a couple of years older than me – with cropped blonde hair and lots of mascara. She was also more energetic. Last night she'd easily matched my frantic need and hadn't worried about exquisitely prolonging the moment, which Eli had ambitiously tried to teach me in one afternoon. But by one in the morning Lene was asking me about Samir and I instinctively knew that she would probably be with him next.

Lene came into the room, barefoot and dressed only in one of my T-shirts. I could see the tendons in her thighs. Eli had a roundness to her, which seemed more feminine.

'Is this your place?' she asked. She stretched her angular body and then lay on her side on the sofa opposite, propped on one elbow, her head resting on her hand.

'I think it belongs to friends of my parents,' I said. I watched my T-shirt ride up over Lene's bony hip.

'Who pays the rent then?' she asked. I didn't know who paid the rent. I wished she would put some clothes on.

'Eli said you were in the camp after what happened. What was it like?'

I looked over her shoulder at a crack in the wall. If she'd asked me that last night, both of us smoking, looking up at the ceiling in the dark, I might have been able to answer. Morning, with the low sun illuminating every corner of the room, wasn't the right time for such questions.

'Samir will be here soon, to take you to the hospital,' I said. She sat up, trying to pull the shirt down over her thighs while appraising me. I looked down at the photo.

'I'll take a shower,' she said. Nowadays we had water four days out of five, and electricity. The end of September had brought with it torrential rains, which had washed away the accumulated dust of the summer bombardment. The subsequent flooding had brought more bodies to the surface in the camp, like the tide used to bring them to the shore during the Civil War, bloated and decaying. We were dressed and breakfasted and waiting for Samir as we drank coffee. Lene looked professional now, like she'd put on a different persona, not just clothes. I struggled to think of something to say to her.

'What will you do with the money?' she asked.

'The money?'

'Yes, the money Eli sent you. It was there, wasn't it?' she said, concerned that it hadn't been in the envelope.

'I don't know yet – I haven't thought about it.'

'Eli said you should go home,' she said.

Did Eli happen to say where home was, I wanted to ask. But I was just annoyed by the fact that Eli had discussed this with Lene, like I was a problem to be solved. I felt as if Eli had been disloyal.

When I opened the door to Samir he smelt of aftershave and cigarettes and I got a fleeting sense of Faris. As he drank his coffee he told me about the new falafel shop he was going to open in the camp, on the main street.

'Even the poor and dispossessed deserve decent falafel with special sauce, my friend,' he said.

Lene gave an overenthusiastic cackle.

'Are you coming into the camp?' Samir asked me.

'I'll make my own way. I have something to do first.'

Samir shrugged and headed for the front door. Lene kissed me on the cheek and annoyingly ruffled my hair while Samir jangled his car keys impatiently in the hall. She didn't say that she'd see me later and I didn't ask her because I wasn't sure I wanted to see her. As I closed the door behind them I realised that I was in the apartment alone for the first time since I believed it was 'blown' by Nabil, but now it didn't bother me. I knew what I had to do.

In the bedroom I rummaged in my duffle-bag and pulled out a battered address book. I put it in my back pocket along with Eli's letter and my passport and headed for the Commodore.

I found Bob sitting with a thin sweaty man in the hotel bar. They were at the table where Stacy used to write on her legal pads.

Bob gestured to the man after greeting me. 'This is Peter – my replacement.' He turned to Peter. 'And this is Ivan, the best interpreter in Beirut.'

I took Peter's limp and clammy hand. His hair was plastered to his forehead. His smile was nervous and brief, his gaze quickly shifting back to Bob, dismissing me as someone he didn't need to bother with. I wiped my hand on my jeans, turning to Bob.

'I need a favour. I need to make an international phone call,' I said.

Bob didn't hesitate, he knew what I was asking. 'You can use the agency phone.' He got up, saying he would take me there. On the way out of the lobby I processed what he'd said earlier.

'What do you mean, replacement?'

'Yeah, I'm going to Managua.'

'Don't tell me: it's in Nicaragua.'

He looked at me to see if I was pulling his leg. 'It's the capital, yes.'

'Isn't Stacy there?'

'She's somewhere in Nicaragua.' We went into a side office in the agency and he pointed out the desk and telephone. 'I'll be in the edit room, in case anyone asks why you're here.' He grinned and closed the door behind him. I took out my address book and found my grandmother's number in Denmark. It would be early morning there, and at that time she would probably be making breakfast for herself.

She answered on the third ring. She wasn't gushing or emotional; it was as if we had spoken last week rather than six months ago. She told me that she'd spoken to my mother only two days before. My parents were worried and had been trying to contact me. No, she told me, I shouldn't go to them, my mother had said I should go to Denmark if I wanted to leave Beirut, because they didn't know what their plans were. They would be visiting Denmark at some point. That sounded like maybe they trusted me to make my own decision. My grandmother asked me if I needed money and I told her I didn't. I paused before telling her about Youssef. She asked me a couple of questions then she was quiet. I waited, listening to the crackles on the line.

'Can you ring me the day after tomorrow?' she said.

'Yes, I'll try.' I hoped Bob would still be here.

'How are you, Ivan?' she asked. It was typical of her to leave this question until last. It was a real question and she wanted a real answer. I looked down, watching my tears pool on the metal desk. 'I don't know who's paying the rent where I'm living,' was all I could think to say.

She laughed and it echoed over the line, like her voice was being bounced around the world.

The space was cramped and the walls pockmarked with bullet holes. Rubble and dust were everywhere. John, however, thought it was perfect.

'This can be the reception area and the examination room could be in here,' he said, pointing into a room the size of a large cupboard.

'There is no room for a desk,' Samir said. He was trying to brush dust from his shirt.

'I'm a doctor, not a businessman. I plan to examine my patients, not write prescriptions for drugs banned in Europe,' said John.

'OK, my friend, I was only saying.' To me Samir said, 'You know he's taking Arabic lessons so he doesn't need you any more.'

This was to be John's new clinic, right in the heart of the camp. He no longer wanted to work in the hospital but was talking about being a step ahead, working with preventive medicine. He was tired of patients coming into the hospital demanding particular brands of pharmaceuticals. 'Ask them', he would tell me, 'if they've been trained as a doctor.' As ever, I resorted to selective translation. His partner in this new venture was Rima, a Palestinian paediatrician fresh from an American medical school. I'd only seen them together a couple of times, but they always seemed to be arguing about medical protocol. Rima had managed to raise the money for this place. In the wake of 'the massacre', as it was now called, all kinds of help had been arriving, including a whole new staff of volunteers at the hospital to replace those who had left. A new set of peacekeeping soldiers had arrived as well, since the Israelis had withdrawn to the outskirts again, their job done. John, however, didn't think his job was done – as well as taking Arabic lessons he was looking for somewhere to live near the camp. Samir couldn't understand this at all; why would anyone want to live like a refugee if they weren't one themselves?

I had just come from speaking to my grandmother for the second time and I needed to speak to John. He was busy giving instructions through Samir to a group of volunteers (mainly elderly women) who had turned up to clean out the rooms. I took his elbow while Samir was giving orders, trying to keep his clothes clean at the same time.

'Asha was mentioned on the BBC World Service,' John said. 'She gave an interview in Cyprus, on her way to Paris. People are just waking up to what's happened.' He clapped the dust from his hands, took his glasses off to rub his eyes.

'I need to talk to you about Youssef,' I said.

'OK.' He shrugged, cleaning the lenses of his glasses with his shirt. We watched Samir digging something from the wall with one of his keys, presumably belonging to a car he no longer drove. I turned to John.

'My grandmother knows a plastic surgeon in Copenhagen who can operate on Youssef. In principle, that is. He's an old friend of hers. The hospital needs his medical records, though. I could only give her a brief description. She's also contacted a charity that will pay for his flight and somewhere to stay but they need some details as well.'

John smiled at me, put his glasses back on. 'Calm down, Ivan. Tell me what you need. But slowly.'

I took a breath.

'Here we go,' Samir said, holding up a deformed bullet between forefinger and thumb, a triumphant grin on his face. 'Kalashnikov,' he said.

I had decided, before coming to Najwa's, not to tell her about Youssef. I sat across from her at the dining table, sipping coffee and fiddling with my lighter. We were inside because of the heavy rain. This was the second time I'd seen her since the slaughter; the first we'd spent on her balcony looking out over the city, not talking much. She'd looked tired then, her limp more pronounced than usual. This time she brought up what she'd failed to before.

'Ivan, why didn't you tell me that you never delivered the passports?' She sounded hurt. My face reddened; it was obvious that she would have found out they hadn't been delivered, yet I'd said nothing at our last meeting. I took a cigarette out of her pack on the table.

'After the massacre I thought nothing would be the same,' I said. 'Nothing seemed to matter any more. I didn't think life would carry on as normal, that people would just go back to work or school. I didn't understand how it was possible to carry on as if nothing had happened.' I studied my unlit cigarette.

'Everything has to carry on, Ivan. You can either lie down and die or you can carry on. It's a choice you make.'

I nodded. I'd believed that anything pre-Sabra would be nullified, the slate wiped clean. But it hadn't been like that. University lectures had started on time, without me. People cooked and ate, had sex, drank, laughed, went to the cinema, made conversation about trivial things. As Najwa said, they carried on. Samir had carried on opening his new café. John and Asha had carried on, even though their paths had been altered by what happened. Asha now had a new purpose and so did John, with his clinic. Najwa was carrying on because she believed that you should redouble your efforts every time you have a setback. Even the survivors in the camp carried on, those that had seen it happen, watched their relatives and neighbours being slaughtered. They were rebuilding their homes, clearing the streets and opening their little shops. I put the unlit cigarette back in its case and picked up my lighter again, flicking it to make sparks.

'I've arranged for this kid, a survivor from the camp, to go to

Copenhagen for treatment,' I said. I put the lighter down and looked up. 'I'm planning to go with him.'

She puckered her lips and I endured an awkward silence. It was worse than if she'd told me it was only to be expected, that they'd known all along I was shallow and unreliable.

Eventually she said, 'I understand. He's your ticket out of here. You think that by choosing to help an individual you can be absolved from the collective struggle. The harder battle is helping everyone, coming up with a solution to the cause of injustice, not just fixing the symptoms.' She leant back and looked through the rain-streaked window. 'Your father understands this.'

I stood up. 'Well, I'm not my father.' I walked to the door and turned to look at Najwa once more. 'He's probably right, my father, but you have to start somewhere, don't you?'

Her mouth formed a little smile.

'The boy's name is Youssef,' I told her.

23

The smell hit me as I woke – sweet and cloying. I opened my eyes to see an SAS stewardess, her manicured hands placing a tray of food in front of me, giving me the lipstick smile she gave everyone. She had to lean over Youssef in the aisle seat and he nudged me as she left to attend the next row.

'Danish women smell nice,' he said in Arabic.

'She's Swedish,' I said.

'They all look the same to me.' He stretched out his cleanly bandaged foot, taking advantage of the extra legroom I'd asked for next to the emergency exit. He tried to make sense of the compartmentalised food on his tray. I looked past the Danish man on my left through the oval window to see the Mediterranean sea beneath us. A tiny shipping tanker sat on the surface but soon disappeared from view. We banked to the right and the sea was replaced by sky, making my stomach lurch. The captain told us we were turning over Sicily, to begin our journey high over Europe before descending to Copenhagen.

I leant back in my seat and closed my eyes. Samir, John and Rima had seen us off at the airport. John and Rima were spending a lot more time together and I could see that their earlier jousting was just a prelude to the real relationship they were now embarking on. I imagined them driving back up the coast road to the camp, Samir working the wheel and gears of his yellow Mercedes like a man infatuated. Last week John had written out a medical report for Youssef, which I got the Danish consulate in east Beirut to fax to the Copenhagen charity funding his treatment. I also left them with a Lebanese passport for Youssef that Samir had hastily sorted out. I didn't know if it was genuine but it cost me most of the money Eli had sent. A few days later a bemused official at the consulate had given me a visa and tickets for Youssef and myself, mine paid for by my grandmother, his by the charity. And here we were, hurtling at 500 kilometres an hour towards a completely different world.

'Make sure he comes back,' was the last thing John said at the airport, pointing to Youssef. 'This is where he belongs. It's his home.'

Youssef was eating his dessert and main course together, taking alternate bites out of each. My grandmother would take to him, I was sure; she preferred children's company to that of adults.

The man next to me opened an *International Herald Tribune*, blocking my view of the window. The front page referred to an impending inquiry in Israel into what happened in Sabra and Shatila while the IDF had been in control of the city, although nobody in Beirut believed they would shoulder any blame. On the inside page was a small picture of Asha being interviewed in Paris; her first stop in a tour of European cities where she planned to educate the world, as she put it, through talks and interviews, giving her account of what happened in the camp. She was also planning to write a book. Her charity had dropped her because, in their view, she had become too political for them, their status compromised by her forthright views on the massacre and who was responsible. Charity people weren't allowed to take sides, they had to be balanced, she was told. John said that being balanced was a sham, that if you could see both sides equally then you were missing some vital fact. The stewardess returned to pour coffee. I declined, finishing the vodka from the miniature.

Youssef examined the small sachet with the moist towelette inside, asking me if it was food. I was going to have to explain a lot of things to him, a lot of trivial and meaningless things that didn't matter in his world and shouldn't matter in anyone's. He wouldn't elaborate on what had happened in the hospital before he was evacuated and I didn't press him, just as I didn't like to be pressed. Youssef, who'd suffered many times more than I could imagine, had less laughter than before, a new wariness in his eyes, a tendency to flinch at loud voices. I was glad to be getting out. It did feel like an escape, but I also felt like I was abandoning people. This went beyond my failed duty to the 'cause'; it was like leaving horribly injured people at the scene of an appalling accident in the futile hope that if you couldn't see it then it wouldn't bother you. The trouble was this: I would always see it; the pictures were branded onto my retinas, the smell embedded in the soft lining inside my nose. Maybe Najwa was right, maybe Youssef was my way out of the broken city behind us. But Youssef was much more than that. It occurred to me (and here was a foolish notion) that my parents could adopt him and in doing so would heal their broken marriage.

'What're you laughing at?' asked Youssef.

'Was I laughing?'

The rattle of the drinks trolley was a welcome distraction. I asked for another vodka and some ice from the stewardess and handed over my two empty miniatures. I didn't get any peanuts this time round, just a less impersonal smile (I liked to think) than before. The Dane to my left had turned the page of the newspaper and I caught sight of a headline with Bob's name in it. I tried to read the article but the newspaper was moving. The man folded it up and handed it to me, smiling.

'Maybe you'd like to read it? I've finished,' he said.

My eyes pricked at this tiny act of kindness. It was strange, lately the smallest sentiment brought me to tears. From the newspaper I learnt that Bob had won an award – something that cameramen give to other cameramen – for his footage of the massacre. Bob was quoted in the piece as saying that 'it is ironic that the footage in question cannot be shown on television due to its graphic nature'.

Youssef had discovered the button that reclined his seat and was seeing how far back it would go. With it all the way back I could see a middle-aged Lebanese woman behind, her make-up over-applied, a large gold cross at her throat. She glared at me and asked if I couldn't control 'the boy'. I turned away, pressing Youssef's seat button so that he was propelled upright and the woman disappeared from view.

'Aren't you going to eat that?' he asked, pointing at my unopened food.

'No, you can have it.'

I took a big mouthful of cold vodka, holding the liquid in my mouth as long as I could before swallowing. It numbed my tongue and burnt my throat.